"I Really Do Want To Know The Man Behind The Flash."

"Good. I hope you find him to your liking," Nate said.

"You're impressing me so far."

He took another sip of his drink. The February breeze blew around them, stirring a tendril at the side of Jen's face. Each time the wind blew, the strand of hair brushed over her high cheekbones and caught on her lips.

He reached up and brushed it back, tucking it behind her ear.

"Thanks," she said, but her voice was softer, huskier than it had been moments earlier.

He couldn't stop touching her skin. He stroked his finger over her lower lip until she pulled back. Her lips were parted and her breath brushed across his finger.

"I can't think when you do that," she said.

"Then don't think," he replied.

Dear Reader,

I'm addicted to the reality TV show *Dancing with the Stars*. I don't know what it is I love about it, but I can't resist watching it every week while it is on and using everyone's phone to text in votes! That show is where the seeds of this story started.

I was thinking about the couples on the show and what if a romance developed between them. From there the story morphed and changed into what it is today. Nate Stern is a former baseball player who has returned to his home in Miami to help his brothers make their club in Little Havana, Luna Azul, the hottest, most desired ticket in town.

Nate has done his part. He loves the playboy lifestyle he has and the fact that he always has the most beautiful women on his arm. Life is good and a lot of fun for Nate, who hasn't been serious about anything since he stopped playing ball. But then he meets Jen Miller, the dance instructor at Luna Azul, and everything changes.

He thinks she's a lot of fun and that they will have a good time together, but things turn a bit more serious than either of them expected.

I hope you enjoy meeting Nate and the other Stern brothers.

Happy reading!

Katherine

KATHERINE GARBERA

TAMING THE VIP PLAYBOY

Published by Silhouette Books
America's Publisher of Contemporary Romance

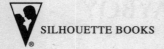

SILHOUETTE BOOKS

ISBN-13: 978-0-373-73081-0

TAMING THE VIP PLAYBOY

Copyright © 2011 by Katherine Garbera

Recycling programs for this product may not exist in your area.

This edition published by arrangement with Harlequin Books S.A.

For questions and comments about the quality of this book please contact us at Customer_eCare@Harlequin.ca.

® and TM are trademarks of Harlequin Books S.A., used under license. Trademarks indicated with ® are registered in the United States Patent and Trademark Office, the Canadian Trade Marks Office and in other countries.

Visit Silhouette Books at www.eHarlequin.com

Printed in U.S.A.

KATHERINE GARBERA

is the *USA TODAY* bestselling author of more than forty books. She's always believed in happy endings and lives in Southern California with her husband, children and their pampered pet, Godiva. Visit Katherine on the web at www.katherinegarbera.com, or catch up with her on Facebook and Twitter.

This book is dedicated to my wonderful daughter
who has started her life as an adult.
I'm so very proud of everything she's accomplished
and look forward to watching her continue to grow
and make a good life for herself.

Acknowledgments

Special thanks to my editor, Charles Griemsman,
for his insight in making this book really shine!

One

The rhythm of Little Havana pulsed through Jen Miller as she parked her car on one of the side streets of Calle Ocho and made her way to Luna Azul. *Blue Moon*...they were rare in real life, almost as rare as second chances, and she was glad for the one that the Stern brothers had offered her by hiring her to be the salsa teacher at their Miami-based nightclub.

The club itself was a rarity. The Stern brothers had created a scandal when they'd purchased the old cigar factory in the heart of Little Havana and turned it into one of Miami's hottest clubs ten years ago. Something that still outraged certain members of the Cuban-American community today.

She pulled the strap of her large Coach bag higher on her shoulder as she walked through the grand entrance of Luna Azul. She stopped as she always did to catch her breath. Nothing said glamour the way the club's

Chihuly chandelier and ceiling installation did. It was a depiction of the night sky filled with a large blue moon. It was also the basis for the club's logo and the colors of the uniform of the entire staff.

Walking through the door each night made her feel as if she was a part of something lasting, and she was very happy to be working here.

The fact that she got to dance again made her even happier. Three years earlier, when she'd made a bad decision based on her heart instead of her head, she'd been banned from competitive dancing.

But now she was back at the barre so to speak and teaching her favorite of all the dances she knew. *The salsa.*

The dance was created by Spanish-speaking people from the Caribbean and even though she was about as white-bread-American as one could be, the dance felt as if it had been created for her.

As she headed into the club, she saw that the main stage was being set up for tonight's performance of XSU—the British rock band that had taken the American pop charts by storm the year before. Her sister and her best friend had both begged Jen to get them tickets for tonight's event and she'd managed to.

She was hoping for a glimpse of the rockers as well but she'd be working during their first set.

The club was divided into several different areas. The main floor in front of the stage was a huge dance area surrounded by high-stooled tables and cozy booths set in darkened alcoves. On the second floor, where she spent most of her time, was a rehearsal room with a small bar and then a mezzanine that overlooked the main club. But the real gem of the second floor was the balcony that opened off to the left and the stage set in the back.

It was there that every night Luna Azul re-created the famous last Friday celebrations held on Calle Ocho. Up there every night was like a feast day for Latin music and dancing. The hottest Latin groups performed there. Regulars and celebrities mingled to the sexy salsa beats of the Latin music.

And she was at the heart of it, Jen thought. She taught the customers how to do the salsa, giving them a little knowledge to help them enjoy the music that much more.

As Jen walked into the rehearsal room, her assistant greeted her with, "You're late."

"I am not, Alison. I'm right on time."

Alison lifted one eyebrow at her. She was funny most of the time but she had a thing for punctuality that Jen simply didn't.

"You're lucky no one has stopped by to check on the classroom."

"Alison, chill. The classroom is ready and we are ready. I brought a new CD with me."

"Which one?"

"Just a compilation of some of my old favorites. I want to have something different for tonight's class."

"What's special about tonight's class?" Alison asked.

"We have T. J. Martinez signed up."

"The third-base player for the Yankees?"

"Yes. And since he's good friends with Nate Stern, I thought we needed to make a good impression." Keeping the club owners and their friends happy was the name of the game.

"Maybe you should have arrived earlier."

"Alison, I don't mind a little ribbing, but you have to drop that. We have thirty minutes before class starts."

"I know. Sorry, I'm bitchy today."

"Why?"

"Marc is leaving for Afghanistan for another deployment."

"When?" Jen asked. Marc was Alison's brother and they were very close. Alison often said that he was all she had.

"Three weeks. I..."

Jen went over and hugged her friend. "He'll be fine. He always is. And I'll help you through it."

Alison hugged her back and then stepped away. "You're right. Now tell me more about the songs we are using tonight."

Jen knew that Alison needed to lose herself in the music so she could forget about her life for a while. Jen wasn't sure she could be as brave as Alison. Having a brother who was a warrior and would always be called to a battle somewhere in the world was hard. She saw it on her friend's face every time Marc got deployed.

The music soon echoed through the empty dance hall as Alison and Jen began their routine. Alison was an okay dancer, though she would never have made it in the competitive world of dance as Jen had. But for Luna Azul she was more than competent.

"I like this," Alison said.

"Great. I want you to add a little more hip twist at the end of the sixth beat like this," Jen said, showing her.

"Very nice, Ms. Miller."

Jen stumbled and glanced toward the door to see Nate Stern standing there.

He was tall—at least six feet in height—and had thick blond hair that he wore cut close to his head. He had the kind of deep and natural tan that everyone wanted and wore his clothes with a stylish panache that she honestly admitted she envied. He had a stubborn-looking jaw with a small scar on his chin from a baseball accident when he was ten.

Why did she know these things? She shook her head. One of the reasons she'd applied for this job was that she'd always been attracted to him. She'd seen his picture in the paper when he'd been a rookie for the Yankees and she'd been smitten.

"Thank you, Mr. Stern. Is there something I can do for you this evening?" she asked.

"I'd like a private word," he said.

"Alison, will you leave us?"

"That's not necessary," he said. "Please join me on the balcony."

She took a deep breath. She hated following orders or letting anyone else be in charge. "Keep practicing."

Alison nodded as Jen led the way out of the rehearsal room and out to the balcony. She tried to be nonchalant but she couldn't help her nerves. This job was literally her last chance in the dancing world. If this didn't work out she was going to have to stop dancing and take Marcia, her sister, up on that secretarial job at her law office. And that was the last thing she wanted to do.

"Is something wrong?"

"No, quite the contrary. I've heard nothing but good things about you and I wanted to come and see for myself."

"So you'll be attending my class tonight?" she asked.

"Yes, I will be."

She almost scowled at him but years of performing for judges enabled her to keep her smile on her face. "That will be wonderful. I believe one of your former teammates is signed up for our class as well."

"Yes, Martinez. I thought I'd tag along and see how you handle having a celebrity in your class."

She almost rolled her eyes. Honestly, did he think she was going to treat T. J. Martinez any differently than she did her other students? "Do you think I can't handle it?"

"I have no idea," he said. "That's why I'll be dropping by."

She was furious but kept calm. "I'm a pro, Mr. Stern. That's why your brother hired me. You don't need to attend a salsa class to ensure I do my job."

He tipped his head to the side. "Did I offend you?"

"Yes, you did."

He gave her a quick grin, which changed that arrogant-looking face of his into a very charming one. "I'm sorry. That wasn't my intent. Celebrities are the key to our continued edge over the other clubs in Miami, and I don't want to chance anything disrupting that."

She nodded. "I understand your concern. I can promise you tonight's class isn't going to damage Luna Azul's reputation one bit. And I will enjoy having you in my class."

"You will?"

"Yes," she said, turning on her heel and walking back toward the rehearsal room. "Because afterward you will owe me an apology for doubting my skills."

His laughter followed her into the hallway and she smiled a bit to herself as she entered the classroom. She had to be in top form tonight and she had absolutely no doubt that Nate would be as challenging in the classroom as he'd been beforehand.

Nate watched her leave, wishing he'd come up here a long time ago. She was funny, spunky and very cute.

Her legs were long—so damned long—and her body was lithe. She was quite a dancer and that was apparent in the graceful way she moved.

He stayed where he was on the patio and stared out at the sky as it darkened into twilight. It was February, and there was a light chill to the night air. The scent of the Cuban food that the patio kitchen was preparing carried on the breeze.

He'd done what he needed to do to keep up the club's image. After all, he was the face of Luna Azul. Funny that a non-Latino would be the face of the hottest club in Little Havana, but the Stern brothers had turned to what they knew best when they'd started their business nearly ten years ago.

Nate was the youngest of the three Stern brothers, Justin the middle one and Cam the oldest. It had been Cam's idea to take the failing cigar factory and turn it into a club. Justin was a finance whiz kid and he'd looked at the numbers and decided if they invested their trust funds into the club, it could make them money.

At the time, Nate had been more interested in his budding baseball career and had merely signed a paper agreeing to the terms. But when a shoulder injury forced him out of the game two years later, he'd been very glad for Cam and Justin's decision to buy this place and open a club. And Nate had quickly found that he had something to contribute to the business.

His A-list contacts from the celebrity world.

As much as he loved to play baseball, he was also a Stern through and through and he loved to socialize. Something that the society pages had noticed when he'd first gone to New York to start his career. And Nate had been careful to make sure he stayed in the news.

He used his celebrity to bring attention to the club and

to stay current. Even though he hadn't played in over six years he was still one of the top-ten most recognizable baseball players.

"What are you doing up here?" Justin asked as he came out of the kitchen area. He was two inches taller than Nate and had dark brown hair. They both had their mother's eyes and their father's strong jaw, a feature all the Stern men had.

"Talking to the salsa teacher. T.J. is going to be in her class tonight and I wanted to make sure she could handle it."

"Jen must have loved that."

"Do you know her?" he asked, feeling a twinge of jealousy at his brother's familiarity with Jen.

"Not well. But I interviewed her for the job and she's very confident of herself. She doesn't like to be questioned."

"Who does?" Nate asked.

"Not me. I have a meeting downtown with the community leaders tomorrow. They want to have their say about our tenth anniversary party."

"How many times are we going to have to prove ourselves before they accept that we are a part of this community now and not going anywhere?" Nate asked.

"They'll never be satisfied," Cam said as he joined his brothers on the patio. "What are you two doing up here? I need you downstairs to talk to the band when they arrive."

"I'm on it," Nate said. "I've got the society reporter from the *Herald* coming. And I'm positive we are going to see Jennifer Lopez tonight. She's in town and her people said she'd drop by. I've got calls in to the internet celeb-site stringers so we should get some good coverage."

"Great. I like the sound of that," Cam said.

"I know you do, that's why I spend all night partying."

"Ha. You do it because you like it," Justin said.

"Indeed, I do. I guess the Stern genes run true in my case. I'm not meant to settle down."

"Like Papa?" Justin asked.

"Yes. I think that's why he and Mom were so miserable," Nate said.

"That and the fact that she was so…cold," Cam added.

Nate turned away from his brothers. Their mother had never wanted children and had done her best to spend as little time with them as she could. It had affected them all in different ways. For Nate, it was that he didn't trust women to really know their own emotions. He always knew that women were going to leave and they always did.

"I guess we all know what to do tonight," Cam said. "How are your talks with the community leaders going?"

"Slow. I invited a few of them to join us for tonight's show so they can see how much a part of Calle Ocho we are."

"Good. Keep me posted," Cam said.

"I will."

Nate and his brothers went back downstairs. Standing in the nearly empty club, Nate glanced around at the decor. It was hard to tell from looking at the place that this had once been a cigar factory.

As a boy, he'd never thought about the future. Once he became a professional baseball player, he'd always just assumed that he'd continue playing until he was in his thirties and then transition to a sportscaster career. But when he'd been injured so young...his dreams had changed and morphed into this.

He wasn't bitter about it. To be honest, he figured he'd ended up exactly where he needed to be and he was very happy about that.

"Nate?"

He turned to see T. J. Martinez standing in the foyer under the Chihuly glass ceiling. "T.J., my man. How was your flight down here?"

"Good. Very good. I'm ready for some action tonight. Ready to mix it up with you."

"Me, too," he said, shaking hands and giving the other man a one-armed hug. "I heard you signed up for dance lessons."

"Mariah insisted that I take them. She said the teacher is the best and that I'd be an idiot to miss out on the classes. Of course, Paul said the teacher was hot."

"You can see for yourself tonight. The first class starts in about thirty minutes. Do you want to have a beer?"

"Yes. I'll catch you up on the team news. There's a rumor that O'Neill is going to be traded."

Nate led his friend to the bar and they chatted about baseball and the players they both knew. It was still early and the club wasn't open to guests yet. But Nate wanted some private time with T.J.

Nate tried to concentrate on the conversation, but his mind kept drifting back to Jen. He didn't attribute much to it, though. Sure she was sexy and spunky—two things he'd always been attracted to. And talking about baseball and his glory days always made him want to go on the prowl.

"Let's go. Don't want you to be late to your class."

"Are you coming with me?"

"Yeah, why not? I haven't been to a salsa class yet and as you mentioned, the teacher is...well-qualified."

T.J. tipped his head back and laughed. Then they finished their beers and headed upstairs. There was no reason for Nate to be in this class except that he wanted to see Jen again. And that was all it took, he thought. That was a perk to being his own boss—he could do whatever the hell he wanted.

He walked in the door of the rehearsal room and Jen glanced up from a turn she was doing. Her hips were swaying and the pulsing sensual beat of the salsa music echoed in the background. He felt the rhythm of it down deep in his soul, and his shoulder started to throb the way it did when something big was about to happen. That old injury was like a dowsing rod for spotting trouble.

Two

The music swelled around her and for once a man distracted her. Well, that wasn't true—she'd been distracted by men before but not like this. Nate Stern was making her conscious of each sway of her hips. She felt the material of her long skirt against her legs and when the side slit parted to reveal her thigh, she felt his gaze on her.

His gaze.

Not another single person in the room was registering for her. *Just him.*

Why?

Why Nate Stern? This had disaster written all over it. She couldn't be attracted to her boss. The last time she had been attracted to someone with authority over her it had ended badly.

Her sister Marcia would roll her eyes and say that

Jen never learned. She had to learn, she thought. She couldn't start over again.

To add to her troubles, Nate's friend T.J. might be a rocking third-base player but he couldn't find the rhythm of the songs she'd played to save his life. It shouldn't be that hard. The strong Latin beat was easy to hear.

Alison was working with some students at the back of the classroom as Lou Bega's "Mambo No. 5" came on. She used her remote to pause the music. This was the song that the class danced to every evening to open the club. Then Alison and Jen would go into the back and come out twenty minutes later to do a flamenco routine.

"Okay. Is everyone ready to show us what you've learned?" Jen asked. "When you signed up for this lesson you probably didn't realize it but you are going to be the stars of the opening number tonight."

There were a few good-hearted groans from the men in the room and a smattering of applause.

"The important thing to remember about the music is that it is sensual. It reflects the rhythm of the night. You should feel it pulsing through you. And don't worry about looking silly, you all look wonderful when you are dancing together."

"I don't think I can feel anything except when someone is going to try to steal third," T.J. said.

"I have to agree, Mr. Martinez."

"Call me T.J.," he said with a charming grin that revealed his perfect white teeth.

"I will. Since you are our celebrity tonight we would like to invite you to lead the conga line into the room and then, of course, have the first dance."

It was their standard procedure to ensure that the classes got the utmost attention. According to Nate

Stern, it was a nice way to drive business to the lessons. Everyone wanted to be in a class with a celebrity.

"I don't think I'm the right guy for that."

Jen smiled at him. "I will make sure you are."

She hit the button to turn the music back on and walked over to T.J. Nate was watching every move she made and she felt as if she had a spotlight on her body.

She gave him a pointed stare and he just grinned back at her. That was when she decided to show the annoyingly handsome man that she was made of tougher stuff than he thought she was.

She'd been dancing since she was thirteen. Let's face it, she thought, there wasn't a time in her life when men hadn't been staring at her body. And tonight…well, tonight she wanted Nate to see her and to want her. She knew she was an okay-looking woman most of the time, but when she danced…she was beautiful.

"I'm not an athlete, T.J., so you will have to tell me, does baseball have its own cadence?"

He nodded. "It might, ma'am, but all I hear is the sound of the bat hitting the ball."

She nodded, trying to think of another way to reach him. How was she going to make this work for him?

"Do you mind if I touch you?"

"Not at all," he said with a grin.

She smiled back at him. Walking around behind him, she put her hands on his hips. "Just stay loose and let my hands move you."

He nodded and she counted the beat of the music under her breath. And then she started to move his hips. He tried to move his feet but stumbled. "Just stay still and learn the beats."

"I don't think that method is working, Ms. Miller," Nate said. "Let me show him how it's done."

She looked at her boss and then put her hands up and stepped back.

But instead of going to T.J., Nate came to her. He put his hands on her hips. "Move so I can feel the rhythm."

His low tone was meant only for her ears and she responded to it. She counted the beat so he'd hear it as loudly as she did inside of her head and then she started to move.

Nate, unlike T.J., moved with an innate grace and natural ability that made dancing with him...well, not work. He put his hands in the proper position for the dance. One hand on her hips and the other holding her hand, his eyes met hers and the other people in the room faded away. In that one moment, Nate wasn't her boss or some local celebrity.

He was her partner, her man, and she let the dance take over. Their gazes met and held as they danced. Nate understood sensuality, and in his arms she realized that she was more than the dance instructor.

The salsa was about heat and sex. It was a seduction, a promise of the evening to come. She felt the barriers she'd been trying to put into place to keep him back start to shake and then fall.

This man wasn't going to let her keep him away if he wanted to be closer. And as the music faded and they stopped moving, she knew he did want to be near to her, or at least she knew that she wanted to be near to him. She wanted to feel his hands on her hips again. To feel his big hand holding hers and watch his dark obsidian eyes as they moved together to the music.

* * *

Nate didn't know why he felt so possessive toward Jen. She was nothing more than a pretty face and an employee but when she'd touched T.J., he'd seen red. And he didn't like that.

Once he held her in his arms, he knew what the problem was. He wanted her. And wanting her was complicating his rather simple plans for an enjoyable evening. But dancing together had also shown him that she was interested in him, too. She watched him, her gaze heated under his as they moved and when the music stopped, he started to pull her to a corner of the room.

But the applause stopped him and Jen bit her lower lip as she stepped back.

"That is what we need to see from everyone," she said. "I'm going to observe you all dancing and then we will be ready for our big debut."

"I don't think I'm going to look like that," T.J. said.

"Don't worry about it," Nate said. "I'll take your place. Unless you have an objection, Ms. Miller."

Jen flushed and shook her head. "You are a very good partner, Mr. Stern."

"Call me Nate," he said.

She nodded. She turned her attention back to the class.

"Why didn't you tell me you had something going with her?" T.J. asked.

"I don't. That was just a dance."

"That was sex on a cracker, man. That was so much more than a dance," T.J. said. "I guess there is no chance for me."

Nate shrugged. It was a connection, and one that he didn't feel all the time, but he knew it wasn't rare. It was just lust. Tonight he was on the prowl. Ms. Miller was attractive and there was something about her that made him curious. Maybe it was her mouth with the full lower lip that he knew would feel right under his. Or her nipped-in waist and long lean dancer's body that he sensed would feel right in his arms.

Hell, he already knew that it felt right here. That she felt right when she moved with him. He wanted to explore it further but he was aware that he was her boss and long-term relationships weren't his thing.

Which could make working together in the future a little uncomfortable.

"What are you thinking, man?"

"That women are complicated."

T.J. laughed. "Understatement of the year. I don't think I'm ever going to figure them out."

"The dances?" Jen said coming over to the two of them. "You should probably stop chatting if you want to master them."

"Sorry," T.J. said. "I think I'm a lost cause."

"I'm not ready to give up on you yet. Maybe Nate can help you with the footwork. He seems to know his way around the dance floor."

"I think I'd rather practice with a beautiful woman than with this retired pitcher."

"Ditto," Nate said.

"Well, I have other students who need my attention as well. And I'm not getting through to you," she said. "Nate, why do you think that is?"

He realized she was being sincere. She wanted to help T.J. and that was the first time he realized that the dance lessons were important to her. He'd been too busy looking at her body and watching her sensual moves to pay attention earlier.

"I'm not sure. T.J. is used to using his body as a blunt instrument and dancing is more subtle, isn't it?"

"Yes, I think you're right. How about a line dance?"

T.J. groaned. "No. My sisters have tried rather unsuccessfully to get me to Electric Slide with them."

She laughed. "Does liquor help? Some people can't let go of their preconception that others are watching them dance until they have a few drinks."

"Not even a keg of beer could relax me," T.J. said. "But I appreciate your trying."

"It's my job."

"And you are very good at it," T.J. said. "I'd put a good word in with your boss but I think he already knows how good you are."

Jen glanced over at him. "Does he?"

Nate nodded. "You are very good."

He realized she was flirting with him just a little and he silenced the voice in the back of his head that had said she was off-limits. Her interest was all the permission he needed to pursue her.

She went back to the front of the classroom and told everyone to take a five-minute break. Then they'd practice the dance they were going to do to open the show one more time.

Nate followed Jen out of the room. She stopped in the hallway when she realized he was behind her.

"I'm sorry that T.J. isn't getting the dance."

"That's fine. You've gone above and beyond trying to teach him."

She nodded. "I'm not sure that you and I should dance together."

"Why not?" he asked, stepping closer to her.

She wrapped one arm around her waist and tipped

her head to the side. The high ponytail that held up her pretty brown hair brushed against her shoulder. He reached out to touch the end of it. Her hair was soft.

"That's why," she said. "I'm starting to forget you are my boss, Nate. And I like this job."

"Dancing with me isn't going to compromise your job," he said. "Luna Azul doesn't have a fraternization policy."

She wrinkled her brow. "I know that. But if something…"

"What?"

"It would be awkward and I really like this job," she said, then turned and walked away. And he let her leave realizing that she was concerned and that he had no idea who she was beyond a pretty girl that he was attracted to.

Jen wanted to just dance into the night with Nate. To pretend that her actions would have no consequences and that she could give in to the powerful attraction and that everything would be fine.

But she wasn't the young girl she'd once been. And she'd paid the price for making a bad decision based on her desires before. She wasn't about to make the same mistake twice.

It didn't matter how nice he'd felt when he'd held her in his arms. Or how right they'd fit together as they danced. It didn't matter.

But it did. She was always looking for a man who made her feel the way that Nate had when they'd danced together. It wasn't just the dancing but how he'd kept her gaze and how they'd just instinctively found the rhythm of each other. That kind of dancing was rare and she wanted to do more than just salsa with him.

She wanted to pull him close while the soul-sex sounds of Santana played in the background.

Stop it.

She needed this job. This was the new Jen Miller. No longer a creature who was ruled by what felt good or right, she now followed the rules. Put family first and was a good girl.

She had to remember that. Marcia had given her a place to stay when she'd needed it and she had promised her sister that she'd changed. That she'd embrace…well, being someone new.

Marcia had always thought that Jen was spoiled and to be honest, she was. She'd had talent from the age of eight. She'd been a dance prodigy and everyone had expected great things from her. And for Jen, those things had come easily.

Crashing at age twenty-six hadn't been in her plans and leaving the competitive dance world behind hadn't been, either. If she wanted to dance—and let's face it, she didn't know how to do anything else—then she needed to keep this job.

And that meant staying away from Nate Stern.

"You okay?" Alison asked, joining her in the hallway.

"Yes. I'm just trying to catch my breath before we go on."

"You and Nate…"

"I know. We have dance chemistry."

"In spades. I think you should capitalize on it," Alison said.

Sure, it was easy for her to say. She didn't have to go out there and dance a sensual dance with a man who was all wrong for her.

"How?"

"Have him come back every night."

"I doubt he has time for that. He's a busy man," Jen said. "Are you ready?"

"I am. Are you going to hang around and wait for XSU to perform?"

"Probably. You?"

"Yes. My boyfriend is meeting me here."

"How's it going with him—Richard, right?"

She nodded. "Pretty good. It's not a forever thing, but we have fun together."

Jen wanted that. Some guys she could have fun with and not lose her heart to. But she'd never been able to do it. Maybe it was simply the way she was wired but she didn't do casual. That's why Nate worried her.

If she could be like Alison and just have fun with him…why couldn't she?

She was starting over—why not start over with her attitude toward men? Why not have some fun?

"How do you keep from caring too much?" Jen asked.

Alison shrugged. "He's not the one so it's just fun. I don't think about anything except having a good time with him. If he's too busy to make it to something I'm doing, I call someone else."

Jen didn't know if she could do that. She wanted to.

"Why?"

"I…I wish I could be like that."

"You don't even date," Alison said. "We've known each other for eighteen months now and you haven't met a guy for coffee."

"I know. I'm just not into the casual scene but maybe I should be. I mean, I don't want to spend the rest of my life alone."

Alison smiled. "Want to come and hang with Richard and me tonight?"

Jen shook her head, then realized that she needed to do something different. "Okay. I'll do it."

"Good. Richard always has his posse with him and there are at least two guys I know who will be interested in you."

She swallowed. "What if I can't do it?"

"Then it's no biggie. They aren't exactly looking for a commitment."

She reentered the rehearsal room. Nate was standing off to one side, talking on his cell phone and she stared at him. And it hit her.

She didn't want to just learn how to lighten up and have fun with any friend of Richard's. She wanted to do it with Nate. He was the only reason why she was even considering changing her ways.

She wanted to spend more time with him but it didn't take a rocket scientist to know that Nate wasn't a long-term dating kind of guy. He always had a new woman on his arm and he was always in the papers. He was an arm-candy kind of guy and she'd never been an arm-candy kind of girl.

Wanting to be with him was understandable. He was hot and flirty. He made dancing feel the way she wanted it to. And he had the kind of dark eyes that she could lose herself in. But that didn't mean that she should pursue this any further than on the dance floor.

Hell, for all she knew he didn't want her for anything other than publicity for the club. Shaking her head, she put on "Mambo No. 5" and got the class ready to conga out into the crowd as she heard Manuel, the deejay for the open-air room, start warming them up.

"Everyone get ready."

"I know I am," Nate said. She felt his hands on her hips and she stumbled over her first step. She stumbled! That never happened.

But Nate caught her, and his hands on her hips as she led the way into the main room were all she thought of. She knew whether it was wise or not she wasn't going to deny herself the chance to get to know Nate better.

Because he was exactly her kind of man.

Three

Nate glanced around the crowded balcony club area and spotted just enough A-listers to make the party interesting. Leaning forward, he whispered in Jen's ear.

"That's Hutch Damien over there. Let's get him in this conga line."

"I don't know him."

"I do. Head over that way," Nate said.

He directed Jen as the line snaked through the tables. She had no microphone on, the deejay did all the talking in this club getting patrons on their feet. She left the conga line and approached the velvet ropes.

"Wanna dance?" she asked in that flirty way of hers.

"I never turn a pretty lady down," Hutch said with a grin. He hopped up and Nate moved back in the conga line to make room for him. The music swelled and Jen snaked through the room gathering up many of the people who all wanted to say they danced with Hutch Damien.

Hutch was a bona fide Hollywood superstar who'd started his career as a teenage rapper, but not with that hard-edged gangster rap—more of a sophisticated and fun sound that had him climbing the pop charts. He had movie-star good looks that he capitalized on to make films that people loved. And he was a genial guy.

Nate and he went way back to before his playing days when they'd both been rich boys at prep school. Since that image didn't jibe with Hutch's public persona of a rapper who made good, they seldom mentioned that fact to anyone.

Jen led them into the middle of the dance floor and then moved off to the side as the music ended and the deejay played "Hips Don't Lie" by Shakira.

Nate left T.J. and Hutch on the dance floor as a group of women came up to dance with them and probably grab a picture or two on their cell phones.

Jen was nowhere to be seen forty-five minutes later. He sent a message to Cam checking in to see if there was anything he needed from him. Then he tweeted about the club, talking up Hutch and T.J. on the dance floor.

He pocketed his phone and sought out his friends in the VIP section. He quickly found Hutch and T.J. and sat down with them. But Nate couldn't stay up here all night; he needed to make sure that there were celebrities throughout the club.

Nighttime was his busiest time but he loved it.

"Where you going?" Hutch asked him when he got up.

"We have a band performing downstairs."

"Not until ten," Hutch said, glancing pointedly at his watch.

Nate grinned sheepishly at his friend.

"There's a girl…" T.J. said.

"There's always a girl for our Nate."

"Yes, there is always a girl. I think you'll like her."

"So she's for me?"

"No," Nate said. "She's mine."

"Fair enough, who is she?" Hutch asked.

T.J. took a sip of his rum and Coke and leaned over the edge of the table, his eyes skimming the dance floor. Jen was in the middle doing a flamenco dance. "There she is. The dark-haired one dressed in red."

"Nice," Hutch said. "She works here?"

"Yes," Nate said, leaning back against the padding of the banquette. "Dance teacher."

"What's her name?" Hutch asked.

"Jen," Nate said.

The fact that he was going to bring her up here said more than he wanted it to. His friends understood that he rarely invited someone who wasn't a part of their group to join them. They were the same way. But Jen was different.

"I like her," T.J. said. "She's funny and knows how to move her body. And this one got jealous when she touched me."

"I am not jealous of you," Nate said.

That was one thing he'd never been. Even when he had been injured and had to quit playing ball he'd never envied those who still played. He didn't waste time dreaming about what might have been. He lived his life to the fullest and if that sometimes meant he had to course correct then he did it.

"I know, man, just joshing with you. Go get your girl before she disappears," T.J. said.

Nate glanced back at the dance floor. Sure enough, Jen and her assistant Alison were taking bows and leaving the club. For the night, he knew.

Nate stood up and walked through throngs of people in the club. He stopped to sign autographs for Yankees fans and posed for pictures with scantily clad women. He kept his smile in place even though he was impatient and wanted to get to Jen.

Cam texted him that there was some kind of problem with the guest list and Nate knew he needed to get down and take care of it, but he was afraid to miss Jen.

Afraid?

He shook his head and began making his way to the front desk instead of waiting for her. He walked down the grand staircase and looked at all the people crowding the dance floor and tried to take some satisfaction from it. This was his life. Luna Azul—the blue moon. Which had been the name of their father's boat when they'd been growing up.

They spent long lazy summer days on that yacht, just his dad and his brothers. Away from their shrew mother's demanding voice. Away from the shore where everyone wanted a piece of Jackson Stern, the PGA golf phenom. Away from the real world on the ocean where they could just be themselves.

And Nate had thought naming the club after that childhood oasis had been a stroke of genius, but then Cam was good about doing those kinds of things. Finding a connection between the past and the present.

He got to the VIP desk just as he caught a whiff of a familiar flowery scent. He glanced over his shoulder and saw Jen standing there.

"Sorry about this. I was told my sister and her friend would be able to get in tonight if I left their names here."

"Of course they can," he said, realizing that this was fate. Jen and he were destined to spend this night together.

Jen had been trying to avoid Nate. Having his hands on her hips during the conga had made her too aware of him. And she knew that she was on the verge of doing something stupid once again so, of course, there'd be a problem with Marcia and her friend getting into the club tonight. And it seemed fitting that Nate would be the one man they'd call to fix it.

"I'm so sorry," she said again.

"It's not a problem," Nate said. He turned to Marcia and smiled at her. "I'm Nate Stern."

"Marcia Miller, and this is my friend Courtney."

"Pleasure, ladies. Give me a few minutes and I will get this straightened out," he said.

He walked back over to the VIP desk and Jen wanted to disappear now while she still could. This was embarrassing. She didn't want to bother him.

"Is this okay?" Marcia asked.

"Yes, it's fine. Nate will take care of it."

"I don't want you to get in trouble," Courtney said.

"I won't," Jen said. She hoped she was right. The club policy was that two comp tickets a month were issued to the employees and she hadn't ever used hers. So she knew that she was technically in the right.

"It's fine," she said again.

Marcia reached over and rubbed her arm. "Nate Stern? Is he your boss?"

"Sort of. You know who Nate is, Marcia, don't pretend you don't."

"I do. It's odd that he seems to be handling operational things. I thought he was a playboy."

Jen shrugged. "That's his image and it works for the club but he's doesn't strike me as someone who's just loafing around waiting for a free ride."

"That's reassuring," Marcia said.

"I know it is."

"How do you know him?" Courtney asked.

"He was in my dance class tonight…one of his friends had signed up and I guess he tagged along to make sure it went smoothly."

"Has he done that before?" Marcia asked.

"No and I've had bigger celebs than T. J. Martinez in the class."

"You had T.J.—"

"Yes, stop drooling, Courtney."

"Ha. I'm not drooling, but he's hot. You have the best job."

"You're just saying that because all you do is Excel spreadsheets all day."

"Very true," Courtney said. "He's coming back."

Jen glanced over her shoulder to see Nate walking toward them. He held up two tickets, which he handed to Courtney and Marcia. "Have fun, ladies."

"We will. Thank you, Mr. Stern," Marcia said.

"Call me Nate. And you should thank your sister. There was just a mix-up with the list you were on," he said.

"Thanks, Jen," Marcia said. "Are you coming with us?"

She nodded.

"Can I have a word before you go in?" Nate asked.

"I will meet you both inside in a few minutes," she said to Marcia and Courtney.

As they left, she turned to Nate. "What's up?"

"Do you have plans for this evening?"

She wrinkled her brow. "I'm meeting my sister and her friend."

"I guess that sounded stupid," he said.

"Just a little bit. Why did you ask?"

"I want you to join me."

"Why?" she asked.

"I think you would be fun to hang with."

She tipped her head to the side to study him. She wanted to say yes and thought about what Alison had said earlier about just having fun. She couldn't ask for someone who knew how to party better than Nate.

"Okay."

"Wow, did you really have to think on it?"

"Yes," she said. "I'm not...I don't make snap decisions."

"I'll remember that. Do you need to check in with your sister?"

"Yes. Why don't you come and hang with us for a little while?"

"That wasn't what I had in mind."

"What did you have in mind?" she asked. She had no idea why she'd agreed to this and she might be in over her head. She should have eased herself back into the dating scene with one of Courtney's financial analyst friends or someone that worked at her sister's law office instead of jumping straight from stay at home every night to Nate Stern.

"You and me burning up the dance floor."

She looked up at him. "I'm not your kind of girl, you know that, right?"

"No, I don't. I think you and I are going to get along very well."

"That's what I'm afraid of," she said under her breath. But in for a penny in for a pound, she thought. She wanted this night and this man so she was going to go for it.

"Come on, Nate. See if you can keep up."

He laughed a full robust laugh. It made her smile just to hear it. He was that kind of guy. The kind that knew how to enjoy life, and she realized she needed someone like that. She needed to learn how to go with the flow.

He took her hand in his big one and led the way into the club, over to where Marcia and Courtney waited. She tried to tell herself that she was in control of this but she had the feeling that Nate was and she wasn't sure what the outcome would be.

Marcia and Courtney left at midnight but Nate wasn't ready to let Jen go yet.

"Stay," he said when they were in the lobby under the beautiful Chihuly glass sculpture depicting the night sky.

"I'm not sure that is wise," she said. "I have to work tomorrow."

"Not until the evening. Stay and play with me, Jen," he said.

"I...okay, why not? What will we do now?"

"There's an after-party for the band. It's up in your court—the rooftop club."

"Okay. But I can't stay past two," she said.

"I won't hold it against you if you change your mind."

"Are you really that confident of yourself?" she asked.

"Of course. I know that you are enjoying yourself and your sister told me that you don't have enough fun."

"She said that?"

"Yes."

"What else did she say?"

"That you were her little sister and she'd hurt me if I hurt you."

Jen flushed. "She's just overprotective. Our mom worked a lot when we were growing up and Marcia was the one who always had to watch me."

"Some habits never die," Nate said. "It's the same with Cam and me."

"I can see that about him. He's like everyone's older brother here."

"He takes care of family. If you cross him...well, I wouldn't."

"Me, either," Jen said.

"Do you know him well?" Nate asked. It seemed odd to him that he'd just met Jen today and that his brother might have known her longer.

"Not really. But he asked me to serve on the tenth anniversary celebration committee."

"Yes, I am to be on that committee, too, so we will be seeing a lot more of each other."

She glanced down and he wondered at her expression. But then T.J. came over and slung an arm around his shoulder. "Buddy, how's it going?"

"Good," he said, realizing T.J. was drunk. He was reluctant to stop talking to Jen, now that he was finally learning a little about her, but T.J. needed him.

"Let's find a table to sit down and chat."

"Nah, I'm making the rounds. Did I tell you that I'm a single guy again?"

Nate shook his head. "I heard it through the grapevine."

"Everyone has," T.J. said.

"I think I see a table in the back that will be nice. Why don't you two go grab it and I'll get us some drinks," Jen said.

"Not a problem, Jen. As soon as we sit down, Steve will send my usual drink order over," Nate said.

"I don't think he'll know what I want, so I will tell him and then join you both," she said.

"Thanks," Nate said, leading T.J. through the crowds to the table that Jen had spotted. T.J. was rambling a little about being single again.

"I hate it, man. I'm not like you. I don't like the party life. I want to go home with the same woman every night. Have a nice little house in the suburbs, ya know?"

Nate patted him on the shoulder. "I do know. It will work out when you find the right girl."

"The right girl? I doubt there is one out there. We don't meet nice girls, ya know?"

Nate started to agree but then glanced up to see Jen walking toward them. He thought that they did meet nice girls in their lives but they never knew how to treat them. And he was torn for the first time in recent memory. He wanted to be more of a gentleman for Jen than he normally was but he had the feeling that it was too late for that. He scarcely remembered how to be a gentleman.

"I don't think guys like you and me know what to do with a nice girl."

"Could be," T.J. said as he looked at Jen. "Did you tell the bartender to bring me another rum and Coke?"

"No, sorry. I told him Coke straight up."

"I need the rum, Jen. I think I could samba better with rum."

"I don't know about that. And I was teaching you the salsa."

"Damn. I guess I'm not impressing you," T.J. said.

"You already have when I watch you play," she said.

"I am a hot third-base player."

"You are a stud on the baseball diamond," Nate agreed.

"I am. I think I'm going to head over to the bar and see if I can get them to add a little rum to this Coke," he said. "Not that I don't appreciate the thought, Jen."

"No problem," she said.

T.J. got up and left the table. Nate watched his friend go and hoped that he'd find some kind of peace in the alcohol.

"Thanks for giving us a minute," Nate said.

"It's okay. I have friends, too. I know how it is when you need some privacy with them," she said.

"Sit down," he said, gesturing to the seat next to him.

"I was thinking I should head out," she said.

"Why? What changed your mind?"

She sat down in the chair next to him perching on the edge of the seat. "This isn't my scene."

"Why not? It's not different than being downstairs with your sister," Nate said.

"Maybe not to you, but this isn't my crowd of people. There are celebs everywhere and people are taking photos with them and I think there are only two groups here."

"What are they?"

"Those who belong and those who are hanging on. And I don't want to be that," Jen said.

She reached over and took his hand in hers and he noticed how delicate her fingers looked with those long pink nails of hers. "I like you, Nate, but this is your world, and being here for just a short time has shown me that I don't belong in it."

"You could if I invited you in."

"I could," she said. "But for how long?"

Four

Nate shrugged. "Life can be pretty crazy."

"I know it can," she said.

"Sit down, Jen. Tell me what brought you here."

She swallowed hard enough for him to see and shook her head. "That's not a good topic of conversation."

"Why not?"

"Because there's a samba playing and I'd rather dance."

And just like that she changed the conversation. He was no longer thinking about who she was and where she'd come from but rather how nice it felt when they'd danced together earlier.

He stood and led her to the dance floor. As soon as they were there he turned and she started dancing. The samba was a very quick-moving dance but he followed her moves perfectly.

When he'd been old enough to notice girls, he'd

realized that they liked to dance and if he knew how—no matter how much ribbing he had to take from his friends—he'd be very popular with the ladies. That had worked to his advantage and he'd liked it.

Jen was a great dancer, her lithe body moving in time with the music, but she also kept eye contact with him and soon the dance felt as if it was just between the two of them.

He found the rhythm and their hips swayed in the same motion. He drew her closer to him as they moved and felt the brush of her body against his. He kept his hand steady in the small of her back even when she would have stepped back.

She looked up at him, confusion and desire evident in her gaze, and he knew that something had just changed between them.

The lust that had been there from the first moment they met was now blossoming into something stronger, something more solid. And as the song built up to the ending, he drew her into his arms and kissed her.

She didn't think of the past or the future. She just lived in the now.

Somehow the night slipped away from her and though she'd meant to leave after one dance, one dance turned into just one more and she spent the night on the floor with Nate. For the first time since she'd been forced to leave the competitive dance world she felt alive.

It bothered her that a man was the reason why. And she knew that this night was a one-off. There was no way she'd ever be with Nate for more than this night. His crowd of friends consisted of people that she read about in glamour magazines and on the internet gossip websites. And though they were unfailingly polite to her, she knew tomorrow they wouldn't recognize her.

"I need a drink," Nate said, drawing her off the dance floor. "You might be used to dancing that much but I am not."

"I didn't notice you falling behind," she said.

"I've got the stamina," he said with a wink. "Plus, I couldn't let a girl out-dance me."

"A girl? Women don't like being called girls," she said to him.

"Ah, I meant it in a nice way. My dad was real old-fashioned when it came to ladies and we were never allowed to call girls women. He thought it was too harsh."

Jen shook her head and had to laugh at that. "I guess it's okay then."

He hugged her close with one arm. They were both sweaty from dancing so much and she liked Nate's musky smell. She leaned in closer for just a second before she realized what she was doing.

"Don't," he said, stopping her by holding her tighter. "I like having you close."

"I like it, too," she said, softly. She looked up into those dark obsidian eyes of his.

"Good. Now how about another mojito?"

"I think water would be better," she said. She was already buzzing a little from the drinks and the dancing. And from Nate, she thought. He went to her head faster than any other man she'd ever been with. Maybe that was because in the past, a man would have had to compete with her dancing career, but now she was simply a woman. And this man…well, he was addictive.

"Water first," he said. "Then mojitos…I don't like to drink alone."

"I'm sure that's not an issue. You always have someone on your arm."

"Not always," he said.

And as he walked away, she realized there was more to the playboy that she'd first suspected.

When he returned to her side, he led her out of the crowded part of the club and behind the stage where there was a roped-off area. There were not a lot of people back here—in fact, it took her a few moments to notice it was just the two of them.

He handed her the water and she drank it down, grateful for it after all the dancing they'd done.

"I love this view," he said, pulling her closer to the railing that ran around the edge of the roof.

She glanced out over Little Havana and toward the Miami skyline. She could make out the bright lights on the Four Seasons Hotel, which was the largest building in Florida. It was a breathtaking view.

"I can see why," she said. "Tell me about this club and how you ended up here."

He arched one eyebrow at her. "I would have thought that was all common knowledge."

She shook her head. "Not really. I mean I know the headlines and the speculation, but I want to know the real story. Why did Nate Stern leave baseball to help run a club in South Florida with his brothers instead of pursuing a career in front of the camera?"

She finished her glass of water and set it down on the wrought-iron table. Nate took her arm and led her farther away from the club sounds as the deejay played Santana. There was a padded bench set amongst some tall trees. The night breeze surrounded them and she felt more comfortable in her own skin than she had in years.

"If I tell you my secrets will you tell me yours?" he asked.

She nodded. "I'm not nearly as interesting as you, but if you want to know about me, I will tell you if you get me a mojito."

"Good."

After a brief trip to the bar, he came back and he handed her the mojito, then gestured for her to sit down. He sat next to her, stretching his long arm behind her on the bench and drawing her closer to him.

Nate didn't like to talk too much about the old days. He did it with guys like T.J. because they expected him to and frankly that was the only thing he and T.J. had in common. The old days.

But reminiscing about what was instead of focusing on what is had never seemed wise to him.

"I think you asked about why I'm here," he said.

"I did. I've always thought...well, since I started working at the club you seem the least likely to actually be happy here in Miami. Why didn't you stay in New York or head to L.A.?"

He shrugged. He'd thought about it. But to be honest, he had been injured and unsure and he'd needed the support of his brothers around him. And frankly, they weren't going to give up their homes to move across the country.

"It just felt right," he said.

She laughed as she turned to look up at him. "I can't believe you made a decision based on your gut. I mean one that would change your life."

"Why not? When I played baseball I made gut decisions all the time." It was one of the things he thought had made him stand out.

"I never thought about it like that."

"Most people don't. So that's it. My brothers were here. I'd invested in the club so I technically had a job, at least on paper, and my sports career was over so I came home."

"You sum it up like you are stating facts," she said, her voice soft and pensive. "Was it really that easy or did you struggle to give up your dream?"

"My dream?"

"Baseball," she said.

He had had a rough patch but had worked through it. "The sad thing about me, Jen, is that I realized I didn't want to be just a baseball player."

"What did you want to be?" she asked, moving closer to him.

He knew he could talk about himself all night with her as an audience. Most people didn't listen well and were just waiting for a chance to talk about themselves but Jen was engaged in what he was saying. He wasn't sure why. Did she really want to know the man he was?

"Famous," he said. "I know, shallow, right?"

"I wanted that, too," she admitted.

He thought she was being kind and trying to make him feel better about his rather shallow goals. Cam always said that Nate was too pretty and that had made him believe he could skate through life. But Nate ignored what his brother said. He'd worked hard to be good at baseball and he'd done it because he thought it would pay off.

In a way, it had.

"Really?" he asked.

"You think I'm joking around?"

"Of course not. But I don't know anything about you.

I know you weren't a baseball player. Our paths would have crossed before tonight."

"Indeed, they would have," she said.

"So?"

She took a deep breath and then a sip of her drink. The mojito was smooth and minty and he saw her savor it as it went down. Since she hadn't lingered over her drink like that before, he suspected she didn't want to talk about herself now.

"Tell me, honey. Your secret is safe with me."

"Honey? You don't know me well enough to call me that."

"Jen, I will before the night is over."

"Isn't that a little presumptuous of you?" she asked.

"No. You are just as interested in me as I am in you."

She nodded. "I am. I hate to say it but I really do want to know the man behind the flash."

"Good. I hope you find him to your liking," he said.

"You're impressing me so far," she said.

He took another sip of his drink. The February breeze blew around them stirring a tendril at the side of her face. Each time the wind blew, the strand of hair brushed over her high cheekbones and caught on her lips.

He reached up and brushed it back, tucking it behind her ear. "There you go."

"Thanks," she said, but her voice was softer, huskier than it had been moments earlier.

"What did you want to be famous for doing?" he asked.

He couldn't stop touching her skin. It was soft, maybe the softest he'd felt in a long time. The women he usually kept company with were concerned about their looks and how they appeared to others—seldom did they let him touch them except in bed when they were making love. But Jen let him touch her face.

He stroked his finger over her lower lip until she pulled back. Her lips were parted and her breath brushed across his finger.

"I can't think when you do that," she said.

"Then don't think," he replied. He tightened his arm along her shoulders and drew her closer to him. Her mojito glass brushed against his chest wet and cold.

She licked her lips and her eyes started to close as he lowered his head. He wanted this night to go on forever but he knew he couldn't sit here on the rooftop another minute without kissing her.

She tempted him on so many levels and he wasn't sure how to deal with a woman who had that effect on him. He wanted to pretend that it was simply the unknown and the curiosity of being with someone who seemed so natural here with him. He didn't have the feeling she was with him because she wanted to meet his famous friends or have her picture in the papers.

And that was a heady aphrodisiac.

Jen was surprised by her reaction to Nate—a non-dancer. She shook her head reminding herself dancing wasn't her life anymore. It still was a shock to think of her world the way it was now.

"I'm sensing you aren't thinking about kissing me anymore."

She pulled back, nibbling on her lower lip. The smell of hibiscus filled the air from the potted plants that were stationed near the edge of the railing.

"No—I mean yes. I was thinking about you. How different you are than the other men I've dated."

"I don't want to hear about the other men in your life," he said, his voice sounding tight.

"Why not? I'm just your one-night girl, right?" she asked. It was imperative to her that she keep her focus here. No matter that Nate was a life-changing man for her. The first guy she'd wanted to kiss since Carlos.

He tipped his head to the side, staring over at her. "Normally, I'd say yes, but I'm jealous, honey. I don't want to hear you talk about other men when you're with me. I want to be the only man on your mind."

She understood that. She was finding herself struck with an uncharacteristic shyness as they sat here alone. It was because he was so different for her...no, he wasn't, she thought. She was the one who was different. She wanted to own this change and not let it own her.

"You are staring very fiercely at me."

"I'm sorry. I just had an epiphany."

He leaned in. "That you should be kissing me?"

"Actually, yes," she said. She should be kissing him. Like Alison had said, life was short and having fun wasn't overrated.

She leaned over and let the shyness that really wasn't a part of her drop away. She was a woman who had always been comfortable in her own skin. She hated that Carlos had stolen that from her.

And Nate was just the man to give it back. Nate Stern was the man she'd regain her womanhood with because she was tired of just existing. It was time to start living again. She glanced up at the full moon and made a promise to herself that starting this moment she would live with no regrets.

She leaned in close and Nate's pupils dilated. "That's more like it."

Yes, it was. She brushed his lips with hers. His were firm and full and when he parted them the warmth of his breath brushed over her. He smelled like the minty mojito and she closed her eyes to just enjoy this moment.

To take from this night the gift it had given her in Nate.

He drew her closer to him. She felt the warmth of his body and slowed this moment down in her mind. The way she did when she was dancing. She wanted to capture every bit of this evening so that when she was old and gray and she told her grandkids about kissing the famous Yankees baseball player she'd be able to do it right.

Then his lips brushed over hers again and she stopped thinking about the future or capturing anything. She thought instead of the way his flesh felt against hers. She thought of the way his lips parted against hers and his tongue pushed past the barriers of her lips and teeth tasting her deep.

The way he took control of the entire embrace, the same way he'd taken control of her night. *Control.* It had always been something she prided herself on but now it hardly seemed worthwhile.

His arms were big and strong as he wrapped them around her and she felt the muscles of his upper arms, the strength in him. Though he was no longer a professional athlete, Nate Stern was still a very strong man.

She put her hands on his shoulders and pushed back to look at his face. The genial smile he'd worn all night was gone and in its place was a fierce expression.

"Too much?"

"Maybe," she said. "Maybe. I came to work tonight expecting everything to be the same, Nate, and now it's not."

"Good. Life should never be predictable."

She shook her head. "Yes, it should. How else do you find your balance if life is always throwing you off?"

He stood up and drew her up beside him. "You find it in the people."

"Family?" she asked as he led the way to the railing.

"Or the city," he said. "Miami never changes. Not really. Not at its heart. Sure there is a different political climate sometimes but for the most part, the beach and subtropical climate encourage a more laid-back approach to living."

His arm around her waist was strong and guiding as he brought them to a stop at the far end of the railing. The sounds of Luna Azul's rooftop club were even more muted here and she looked out over Calle Ocho and Little Havana.

"Did you grow up here in Little Havana?"

"No. I grew up on Fisher Island."

"Oh," she said. She'd known that from the reading she'd done on him and his brothers before she'd taken this job. But the way he spoke about Miami, well, it had sounded as if he knew the city. The city she'd grown up in. Being middle class—okay, lower-middle class—she'd grown up in a far different neighborhood than the affluent community of Fisher Island.

"You?"

"Here in the city."

He tipped her head up. "Then you know what I mean."

She closed her eyes and thought of the city and the rhythms of the Calle Ocho. She thought of the struggling lower-middle class who still knew how to have fun and remembered birthdays spent on the beach.

"Yes, I do."

"Show me what you see," Nate said. He moved around so that he stood behind her. His chest and front pressed along her back, his hands settling on her waist and his chin resting on her shoulder. "Show me your city."

She started to point out the places she knew and what she heard when she was there. "Each part has a different rhythm, a different feel to it."

"Like dancing?"

"Just like dancing. Some of it is hip and current, other parts sensual and emotional, some parts are the blues… the vibes all resonate around me."

"Show me," he said again, turning her in his arms and kissing her the way he had when they were sitting down. But this time he pulled from her so much more than a response to a kiss. He pulled out the song that she heard in her head. The song that was the very heart of who she was.

And she shared it with him with the sensual undulation of her hips. And the way she rested the curves of her breasts against the firmness of his chest.

Five

The sun was just coming up over the horizon when they arrived at his penthouse apartment in a skyscraper downtown. Nate had seldom enjoyed an evening as much as he had this one and he knew it was due to the fact that he was with Jen.

She stood in his foyer looking sleepy but happy and in this moment, Nate felt as if the night was a success. Somewhere between all the kisses and caresses he'd realized that despite the fact that she was a dancer and spent her life with people staring at her body, Jen was shy about letting anyone touch her too much.

He pulled her into his arms. He didn't care about the city or what she thought of it, he wanted her. Had wanted her from the moment she'd sassed him in the club earlier. And the entire night had just reinforced that longing.

"I like this place," she said as she walked across the Italian marble floor.

She stood in front of the floor-to-ceiling glass windows in his living room. "This view..."

"Incredible, isn't it?" he asked, coming to stand behind her. He put his arms around her and drew her back against him.

"I had fun tonight," she said. "I didn't expect to."

"Why not?"

"This wasn't my best day," she said.

"I thought you enjoyed yourself," he said, leading the way to his modern kitchen. He directed her toward one of the high-backed stools at the counter.

"Tonight has been fun. But it started out worse...I'm tired, so I'm not making sense. I meant to say you made a bad day better."

"I'm glad. What was bad about it?"

"Just some news I was hoping would be different."

"What news?" he asked as he started gathering the ingredients for omelets from the refrigerator.

"Remember earlier tonight when you asked me about my secrets?" she asked. She didn't look up at him but instead traced a pattern on the Mexican tile countertop. Her finger just ran across the pattern over and over again. He was struck by how long her fingers were. He wondered what they'd feel like on his skin.

"I do, indeed. Does the bad news have to do with your secrets?" he asked. He really hadn't thought she was hiding much. She was a dancer and a choreographer. What kind of secrets could she have?

"Yes, it does. I don't know what you know about my past," she said, glancing over at him.

"Not too much. If I had to guess I'd say you were a dancer."

"You'd be right on the money. Dancing has been my life for as long as I can remember. And I made a mistake a few years ago and haven't been able to compete since then," she said.

"What kind of mistake?"

"One that involved a man," she said. Her eyes were wide and weary as she watched him and he kept his face neutral.

"It's funny, Jen, but a woman ultimately led to my change of profession."

"Really?"

"Yes. When I was injured I had been engaged and while I was recovering, she decided to move on to a different player."

"I'm sorry."

"I'm not. Obviously, we weren't going to be happy together. I learned a very important lesson from her, one I haven't forgotten," he said.

"What was that?" she asked.

"That I'm not cut out for marriage," he said.

"To her," Jen said. "Why did you tell me?"

"So you wouldn't feel like you were the only one to make a mistake because of love. What happened with your 'mistake'?"

"I was forbidden from competing in the Latin dance competitions. I filed an appeal," she said. "After a lengthy review, the verdict stands and I'm still not welcome to compete." Her shoulders fell. "I'm never going to compete again."

"That's okay. You are going to do other things," he said. "At the club every night you share your love for Latin music and dances with someone new. That has to count for something."

She shook her head. "It's not the same."

"No, it's not. But that is life, isn't it?"

"Yes, it is. I am still struggling to figure out where I'm going to fit in without competition."

"How long has it been since you competed?" he asked. He thought she'd been working at Luna Azul for at least a year.

"Three years. I filed a protest as soon as it happened. And I don't want to sound like I'm full of myself but things usually work out for me. I just expected this to do the same."

"My dad used to say that everything happens for a reason," Nate said, hearing his father's voice in his head. "We might not understand the reason but it's there."

She tipped her head to the side and studied him. "Do you believe that?"

"Yes, I do. I'm going to tell you something I don't let most people know," he said, leaning across the counter so that their faces were close.

"What is that?"

"I couldn't have been as content playing baseball as I am with the life I'm living now."

"Really?" she asked, sounding a bit skeptical.

"Truly. I get to see my brothers every day. I'm paid to entertain my friends and make sure that people have a good time. Is there a better job in the world?"

She nodded. "I see what you mean. I do love dancing and I'm able to do that every night."

She got a far-off look in her eyes and he knew there was more to the story than she was letting on. "I guess I had gone as far as I could in that career. It was time for something new."

"And you get to spend the morning with me," he said.

"Wow, Nate, don't sell yourself short," she said with a laugh.

"I never do," he said, kissing her.

* * *

Nate's advice made sense and she liked the way he gave it out effortlessly and didn't try to pretend that he had all the answers. He was more than she'd expected him to be, but then he'd been surprising her all night. She should be used to it.

"I'm not really hungry," she said at last. She hadn't come back to his place to eat and they both knew it.

"I'm not, either."

He came around the counter and drew her to her feet. "Want to see the rest of this place?"

"Yes, I do."

He led the way down the hall to his bedroom. On the walls were exquisite pictures in bright colors that reminded her of Mexico City. His home was very modern and now. But it wasn't a cold, modern decor, it was very warm and inviting and Jen was amazed that she felt so at home here.

She drew him to a stop under a portrait of him wearing a Yankees cap. "When did you take this?"

"Season opener. My dad wanted it…he was so proud of me for going pro. He came to every game if it didn't interfere with his playing schedule. This hung in his bedroom at our home on Fisher Island."

"When did he die?" she asked.

"Two weeks after I got injured. He didn't know I'd never play again," Nate said. "I'm glad."

"I think he'd still be proud of you," she said. She knew that her parents would have been proud of her no matter what she did. Marcia always said that parents just wanted their kids to be happy. Usually she was referring to her own seven-year-old son Riley.

"I'm not sure. Why am I telling you all this stuff?" he asked.

"People tell me things," she said. "I think I look like the girl next door and people just feel comfortable with me. You probably do, too."

"Girl next door? What do you mean by that?"

"Just someone comfortable. You know, the kind of girl you can tell your secrets to."

"You called yourself a girl."

She mock-punched his shoulder. "I do it all the time, but that doesn't mean I like hearing a man call me a girl."

He smiled. "Just when I think I have you figured out you do something else to surprise me."

"I hope I'm not so easy to figure out," she said. No matter that she told him about her dancing suspension. She usually played her cards closer to her chest. But to be honest, she had no idea how to deal with this life now that she had no direction. And opening up to Nate felt right somehow.

"You're not. You are very complex," he said, pulling her into his arms. "And very beautiful."

He leaned in close and whispered in her ear, telling her how sexy he found her body and how much he wanted to touch her all night. His breath was warm and she liked hearing what he said.

He made her feel like she wasn't incomplete. And that was it, she thought. Since she'd had her appeal denied, she realized that she'd felt broken, but here in Nate's arms none of that mattered.

She twined her arms around his neck and lifted herself up to kiss him. His mouth moved hungrily over hers and she lost herself. His hands skimmed down her back and settled on her hips. He pulled her closer to him.

The feel of his strong, muscled arms around her

made her feel very delicate and feminine. She had never been with a man who felt like Nate did. He was strong, muscled, his body still in shape from years of being an athlete. There was no way for her to pretend he was anyone other than Nate Stern.

Her blood flowed heavier in her veins as he moved his hands over her. She knew that Nate was in control of this embrace. She was letting him set the tempo and as much as she wanted him, she wasn't ready to take the lead in anything between them. He lifted her off her feet.

"Wrap your arms and legs around me," he said.

She held tight to him as he walked them into the bedroom. He sat down on the edge of the king-size bed. His hands roamed up and down her back as she looked down at him.

He tipped his head up and kissed her. There was passion in the kiss but also a note of tenderness and it was the tenderness that won her over. She held his face in both of her hands and plunged her tongue deep into his mouth. He reciprocated, tangling one of his hands deep in her thick hair.

He held her tight as passion overwhelmed her.

He leaned back and she straddled him on the bed. He palmed her breasts, cupping and fondling them gently. She undid the buttons of his shirt and he slowly drew her blouse up her torso. She liked the sensation of the cloth against her skin. She stopped what she was doing and tipped her head back, enjoying the moment.

His hands were warm against her flesh and he draped the fabric over the top of her breasts so that it hung there. His big hands encircled her waist and drew her down toward him.

She felt the warmth of his breath against her nipple

a moment before his lips closed around it. She held his head again as he suckled her through the lace of her bra. Everything in her tightened as he caressed her.

She tried to reach behind her to unfasten the bra but he held her wrists. "Not yet. I want to do it this way."

"You do?"

He nodded.

She reached between their bodies and found the hard ridge of his erection. She stroked her hand up and down over him through the fabric of his pants.

"Do you like that?" she asked as he arched his back and moved his hips against her stroking hand.

"Very much. Want to get naked?" he asked, with a grin.

"More than you can imagine, but I thought you wanted to wait."

"Touché," he said, snaking his hands around her back and undoing the clasp of her bra. He pushed the fabric up out of his way and then lifted her off his lap. "I can't see you in this light."

He rolled over and turned the bedside light on. "Take your blouse off."

She removed it and her bra as he took off his shirt. The muscles she'd noted when he'd carried her were visible now. His pecs well-developed, his arms all sinew and strength.

He had a light dusting of hair on his chest and it tapered down to a thin line, which disappeared under his belt into his pants.

She stood up next to him. She caressed him from his neck down his chest. Swirled her fingers over his pecs and thumbed his flat nipples before letting her touch go lower.

He stood there and let her explore him. She liked the

way the hair on his chest abraded her palm. She liked the warmth of his body and the strength in him.

She leaned down and let her lips follow the path that her hands had. She nibbled on his neck and felt his hands on her back, sliding up and down. Rubbing over her spine and then moving slowly back up.

She felt him lower the zipper at the side of her skirt and the fabric pooled around her feet. She stood there in her flesh-colored bikini panties. He took her hands in his and held her arms away from her body.

"Someday, I'm going to ask you to dance for me when we are alone," he said.

"I might," she said. "But only if you do something for me."

He nodded and brought his hands to his belt. Slowly he undid it and drew it through the loops on his pants. He tossed it on the floor and then pushed his pants down. "Come here."

"No, you come here," she said.

He arched one eyebrow at her and came over to her. She pushed him down on the bed and gave him a minute to get situated before she came down on top of him. She put her hands on his shoulders as she straddled his hips. She rubbed her feminine center over his erection and felt his flesh flex under her.

"Like that?" she asked.

"Hell, yes."

He gripped her hips and rubbed her over his penis. She tipped her head back as she enjoyed the sensation, which spread out all over her body. Gooseflesh spread down her arms and her nipples tightened.

Nate leaned up and ran his tongue over her nipple and her flesh tightened even more. She shifted her shoulders so that her nipple brushed over his lips before he closed them around it and suckled her deeply.

"I want you," Nate said.

"I know," she whispered. She leaned down over him, rubbing her self against him.

"Why aren't we completely naked?" he asked.

"I…I don't know. I thought you'd like to do the honors."

"Indeed, I would," he said.

He pulled her flush against his body and rolled them to their sides. Then his hands swept down over the curve of her hips. He tugged on the waistband of her panties lowering them slowly. She lifted up to help him and he pulled them down her legs and tossed them on the floor.

"Lay on your back," he said. "I want to remember how you look on my bed."

She liked that idea, so she rolled over. "How do I look?"

"Like a siren beautiful enough to tempt a man from the sea. To tempt me into dangerous waters."

She lifted her knee up and parted her legs. "Surely I'm not dangerous, Nate."

He shook his head. "You are the kind of danger I love—highly addictive."

He stripped his own underwear off and stood next to the bed completely naked. His erection was long and wide and she bit her lip at the thought of having him inside her.

She reached out and touched the tip of his shaft and it became even more engorged with blood. She ran her finger around the edge of it and then wrapped her hand around him.

His hips canted toward her. He had one knee on the bed and his hands on her thighs before he pulled back.

"Damn. Are you on the pill?"

"Yes," she said. "I'm a dancer...I can't afford to get pregnant unless I am ready to retire."

"Good. Then we don't have to worry about a condom," he said.

"Actually..." she said. "I want you to wear one. You are a bit of a player."

She hated to say that especially since they were so intimate right now but she wasn't going to be stupid about her own health.

"I guess you have a point. Give me a second," he said. He left the bed and was back in less than a minute.

"Come to me."

He nodded and came down on top of her. But he supported his weight with his elbows and his knees at first, hovering over her. He kissed a path from her neck down to her sternum and then nibbled at her belly button.

Everything inside of her clenched as moisture pooled between her thighs. She wanted him inside of her. She didn't want to wait another minute but she also enjoyed what he was doing too much to ask him to stop.

He slid lower between her open thighs and she watched him as he looked down at her body. He parted her nether lips and leaned in to stroke his tongue over the bud at her center.

The touch of his tongue was electric and she jerked on the bed. No man had done this before. She wasn't sure she liked it at first but Nate took his time lapping at her most sensitive flesh until she put her hands in his hair and held him to her. She was so close to an orgasm and she didn't want him to move...not yet.

He slipped one finger into her and she moaned. Her legs moved on the bed, and around his head. It was too much as he added a second finger and continued to stroke inside of her.

"I'm going to come," she said.

He lifted his head and looked up the expanse of her body at her. "Do it."

He lowered his head once again and she felt the careful scrape of his teeth against her intimate flesh. Her muscles tightened and her climax roared through her. She clutched his head to her body as her hips jerked off the bed.

She kept spasming and he kept his hand between her legs as he slid up her body. He positioned himself between her thighs and waited poised at the portal of her body for a minute. The feel of the tip of his manhood there made her crave more of him.

She put her heels on the bed and lifted her hips trying to take him deeper but he shook his head. "I want this to go slowly."

"I want you inside me, Nate. Now."

Taking his time, he slid inside her body inch by inch and once he was fully seated he waited until she moved her hips and then he started thrusting slowly inside. He felt so damned good inside of her.

He thrust more quickly and his hands tightened on her hips. He brought his mouth to her neck and kissed her there whispering dark words of passion in her ear until she felt like she was going to come again. She reached down and clutched his buttocks, drawing him closer to her with each thrust. He moaned her name as she came again.

This time was so much more intense. She couldn't stop her body from thrusting up against him. His hips began to pump frantically into her and then he called her name as he came.

He held her in his arms, rolling to his side when he was able to. The sweat dried on their bodies and Jen looked up at him in the light cast by the bedside lamp. That was the most intense experience in her life. And Nate Stern was not only essentially a stranger but he was also effectively her boss.

What had she done?

Six

The morning sunlight was muted through the roman shades on the windows. Nate normally didn't like for a woman to stay too late in the morning but he was in no hurry for Jen to leave. She lay cuddled next to his side with her head resting on his shoulder and her arm wrapped around his waist.

The soft exhalation of her breathing stirred his chest hairs and he felt something close to contentment with her in his arms. She looked peaceful and ethereal in her sleep.

The sheets pooled low on her waist revealing the curves of her breasts and the slope of her hip. He reached out to trace the line of her body. She was a dancer, long and lithe yet still had a feminine curve to her.

What was he going to do with her?

He should be hustling her out of his bed and instead he wanted to draw her closer and lay here until she woke.

Then he wanted to make love to her and spend the day with her.

He stared down at her trying to figure out what it was about Jen that was different. Part of it was the obvious fact that she wasn't in his crowd and seemed to have no desire to use his connections to get anywhere.

She was the first woman he met that needed nothing from him. To be fair, she worked for him at the club, but that had nothing to do with him personally.

"Why are you staring at me?" she asked, shifting on to her back.

"You are incredibly pretty," he said.

She seemed to get more beautiful as he spent more time with her. He loved the fuller curve at the bottom of her lip and how she pursed her lips when she thought he was joking with her.

"I'm a real Mona Lisa," she said.

"You are a very interesting woman, Jen," he said, leaning down to kiss her. "I could look at you all day."

"I'm not sure—"

"Don't think about it," he said, putting his finger over her lips. "Let's spend the day together and enjoy the time we have."

"What will we do?" she asked. "I have to be at work at five."

"Me, too," he said. He rolled over on his back and reached for his iPhone, which was on the nightstand. He pulled her into the curve of his body. She cuddled close to him the way she had when they'd been sleeping and he liked that.

He opened the weather application on his iPhone and saw that it was going to be a perfect day for sailing. "Want to go out on my yacht?"

She laughed. "Do you say that to all the women you date?"

"Yes. I don't have etchings to show them so instead I invite them to go boating."

"I'd love to go out on your yacht. But I don't have a change of clothes to wear," she said.

"There's a boutique in the lobby of this building," he said. "What size do you wear?"

"Um…six," she said.

"I'll order some clothing for you."

"No, that's okay. I think I'll go home and shower and change. I can meet you at the marina later," she said.

He shook his head. "That won't do. I want to spend the entire day with you."

"And you're used to getting what you want?" she asked.

"I am," he said. He didn't always get what he wanted but she didn't need to know that right now.

"Why should I stay?" she asked.

"I asked you to. I want to get to know you better," he said.

"I guess I can't argue with that," she said.

"I'm very glad to hear that. My housekeeper should be here now. What would you like for breakfast?"

"I'm a light breakfast eater," she said.

"How about a croissant and fruit?" he suggested.

"That's fine."

"Good. You go shower and I'll take care of every detail for our day. You can use my robe until your clothes arrive."

"Thank you," she said. He kissed her before she got up and watched her walk across his bedroom.

As soon as she was gone, he focused on organizing the day for the two of them. He kept himself busy so he wouldn't think about making love to her again. He felt a bond growing between them. And that was dangerous for him. He should have hustled her out the door when he had the chance but he wasn't really good with should-haves.

He dressed in a pair of casual pants and a T-shirt and walked out into the main living area of his apartment. The sun shone over Biscayne Bay and glistened on the lap pool on the terrace.

"Good morning, sir," Mrs. Cushing said as he entered the room.

"Morning, Mrs. Cushing. I have a guest for breakfast and we'd like something light—fruit, croissants, coffee and juice. I think we'll be ready to dine in about thirty minutes on the patio."

"Certainly, sir."

"I'm expecting some packages from the boutique downstairs. Will you check and make sure they are here before breakfast?"

"I will. Anything else, sir?"

"I won't need you for the rest of the day once you serve breakfast. I hope you will enjoy a free Saturday."

"I enjoy all the free days you give me," she said.

"I'm glad. Thank you."

"You're welcome, sir," she said.

Nate went back into the bedroom and heard the shower running. He was tempted to join her in there but wanted her to have some time to herself. And if he joined her, it would be more than sleeping together. More than a one-night stand. Besides he wasn't building a relationship with Jen no matter how much it might seem like he wanted to do just that.

While Nate showered, Jen sat on the rooftop patio of his home next to the lap pool looking out at the glittering

Biscayne Bay. The view afforded by this condo was breathtaking but to be honest, it wasn't the stunning vistas that were on her mind. It was Nate Stern.

She knew that yesterday had been tough—the International Ballroom Dancing Federation had denied her appeal. She'd never dance again. But to come home and spend the night with him...why had she done that?

She didn't regret it. She tried not to have regret in her life because as Marcia said, regret was useless unless a lesson was learned from it.

Her BlackBerry pinged and she glanced down at the screen to see it was a text message from Marcia.

Are you okay?

She took a deep breath and thought about what she was going to say to her sister before she texted her back.

Fine. I'm at Nate's. Sorry I didn't call sooner.

There was no reply for what seemed like forever and then her phone rang.

"Hello, Marcia."

"Jen, what are you thinking?"

Jen had asked herself the same thing more than once and she still had no idea. "I don't know. I do know that my old life is completely gone and it's time to try something new."

Marcia sighed. "Sweetie, just be careful. Deciding to have a different attitude isn't as painless as you might think."

"Was it like that for you?"

"When Riley was born?"

"Yes," Jen said.

"Sort of. I knew before he was born that I was going

to be raising him alone and that wasn't what you and I were taught was a good family for a child."

"I know. But Riley has turned out great," Jen reminded her sister.

"He has, but it was hard. And I had no choice with him. From the moment I learned I was pregnant I wanted him. This change for you is your doing."

Jen didn't point out that so was her sister's pregnancy. Marcia was eighteen months older than her and thought she was always right.

"I am taking control of my life," Jen said. "Yesterday when I got that letter continuing my suspension and realized that the old life I had was completely closed to me, I thought it's time to figure out who I am."

"And being with Nate is going to help?" Marcia asked.

"I have no idea, but I was impulsive for the first time in my life. You know I've never done anything that wasn't to forward my dance career from the time I started dancing. Literally, Marcia, I can't remember a time when dance wasn't the focus of my life."

"I know. I remember how dancing took up every second of our lives."

"I'm sorry," Jen said. "I know that wasn't fair to you."

"You're talented, kiddo. I forgave you a long time ago for being so good at it."

Jen laughed. "Thank you."

"For forgiving you?"

"No, for being my big sister and loving me."

"Not a problem. Where is Nate?" Marcia asked.

"Showering. I'm on his patio overlooking Biscayne Bay. The view is incredible."

Jen stood up and walked around the pool and sat on

one of the padded benches next to the water. "It's like I'm not even in the city."

"Enjoy being in that different world," Marcia said. "But remember that being impulsive always has consequences. And eventually you are going to have to come back to earth."

"I will. I'm working at five today but will be home by ten tonight."

"I'll see you then. Are you off tomorrow?"

"Yes. Why?"

"Riley wants to go to the park with his favorite auntie."

"Tell him it's a date," Jen said and hung up.

"Who do you have a date with?" Nate asked, stepping out on to the patio.

She hung up the phone and then turned to look over her shoulder at Nate. "Riley...my nephew. We usually spend Sunday together at the park. I take him for the morning and let my sister sleep in. It's the one day a week she can."

"I want to hear more about your family," he said.

The housekeeper brought out their breakfast and then left. Nate gestured for Jen to come sit down at the glass-topped table.

When she was seated next to him, he poured them both some coffee. "What does your sister do?"

"She's a lawyer," Jen said.

"So she's smart like you," Nate said. "What kind of law does she practice?"

"Family law. She does divorces and custody hearings," Jen said. "I don't know how she does it, but she really likes it. Her job is really demanding and with Riley she has no free time."

"Where is Riley's dad?" Nate asked.

"He's not in the picture. Having kids and a family wasn't what he wanted. But Marcia did, so they went their separate ways."

Nate put his fork down. "I don't understand men like that. I know guys who make that same decision. But a child is a part of you...I couldn't abandon a part of me," he said.

Jen was surprised to hear him say that. Surprised that family meant as much to him as it obviously did. "Family is important to you."

"Hell, yes. You know how you talked about not being a dancer anymore and not being sure who you were without that?" he asked.

She nodded.

"I was the same way with baseball and I saw a lot of 'friends' drop me when it was clear I wasn't going to be able to play anymore. But my brothers—they just said come home and we will do something together. Something that will be an even bigger adventure than baseball was."

"Did you regret it?" she asked.

"Not once. I wouldn't be here with you now if not for that long-ago injury."

She wanted to pretend that his words didn't make her heart melt but they did. She knew then what Marcia had warned her about. The consequences of spending the night with Nate—and now this day with him—were that she'd forget he was an impulse. She'd forget they were just supposed to be having fun and maybe start caring for him more than she should.

The sea breeze blew across the deck of the boat, stirring Jen's hair around her face. She wore a pair of dark cherry-red round-frame sunglasses, which went perfectly with the sundress he'd bought for her. It was a deep navy blue with a V-neck and a tie at the back. He'd gotten her a light sweater to wear over it since it was cool on the water.

She sat at the stern of the boat and he watched her from the flybridge. Ordinarily, he'd have a crew onboard but today he wanted to be alone with Jen. To have her completely to himself. He knew that this would be the only day they'd spend together like this for a while. He had a busy social calendar and it was important to the club that he always have his picture in the society pages.

And unfortunately, Jen didn't have the kind of headline-grabbing presence he needed. But he couldn't regret spending the day with her. She was what he needed and he was enjoying every minute of it.

When they were out to sea and out of the shipping lanes, he dropped anchor and joined her at the back of the boat.

"This is so nice. I haven't been out on a yacht before."

"Do you like the ocean?" he asked.

"I do. But there never seems like enough time to just take a day and go out on the water like this. Thank you, Nate."

He sat down next to her. "You are very welcome."

"Why did you bring me out here?" she asked.

"I wanted you all to myself. Away from the distractions of the club and of our real lives."

She nodded. And he wondered what she was thinking. He couldn't see her eyes behind the lenses of her dark glasses. And when she got quiet, he felt as if she retreated to someplace he couldn't follow.

"I saw a picture of you on this yacht…sitting right here. I think it was in *Yachting Magazine*."

He nodded. "With the Countess De Moreny. She was thinking of buying one of these Sunseeker boats and I let her try mine out."

"You looked quite friendly with her, intimate," Jen said.

"I was. I like Daphne," Nate said. "Is that a problem?"

Jen shrugged. "You seemed almost too perfect last night and today and I have to remember that you are a player. That I'm not some woman you are just going to fall for. Please don't let me forget that."

He knew that he was dealing with someone who wasn't used to the world he traveled in. And he'd already decided that was part of the reason she was so appealing to him. But he didn't want to have to remind her not to care about him.

He wanted her to care.

He wanted her to think about him all the time and when they were apart he wanted her to try to get back to him. And he knew that wasn't fair.

"I'm not playing with you, Jen," he said at last.

"I never thought you were. For me this was a crazy dare. Something that I probably wouldn't have done at any other time, but for you, this is your life. A different woman every night and a lot of fun. I have to remember that we're essentially two very different people," she said, pushing her sunglasses up on her head.

He saw fear and caution in her gaze and he knew that she was being as honest with him as she could be. She wanted to be sure she didn't get hurt, and he didn't want her to be hurt.

"I would never do anything to hurt you," he said.

"Not intentionally," she said. She slid out of the

padded bench until she stood on the deck. "Give me the tour of this floating luxury craft. I want to be able to tell my nephew all about it."

He let her change the subject because there was nothing more he could say to change her mind. He knew he'd simply have to do whatever it took to make sure she knew how important she was to him. He wasn't about to let her waltz out of his life easily.

"Does Riley like the water?"

"He loves it. He's an avid deep-sea fisher...well, as avid as a seven-year-old can be. But he always talks about being out on the ocean. Marcia and I take him out on a fishing trip at least once a month," she said.

"What has he caught?"

"He got an eighty-pound, yellow-fin tuna the last time we went out. It took both Riley and the captain to bring that thing in. Want to see a picture?"

"Yes, I'd like that."

She pulled out her cell phone and hit a few buttons. A minute later she turned the screen of the phone toward Nate and showed him a little boy standing next to a fish that was almost taller than him. The boy had thick dark hair and, he noticed, Jen's eyes.

"He looks so proud," Nate said.

"He was. Marcia had the fish preserved and mounted and it's hanging over his bed now," she said. "I don't think I have a picture of that in here."

Nate put his arm around her and took the phone from her. "How about a picture of you and me on the yacht so you can show him when you get home."

"That would be nice," she said.

Nate wrapped his arm around her waist, and Jen put her head on his shoulder as he extended his arm out far enough to get both of them in the picture.

"Smile now," he said, taking the picture. He looked at the screen and saw that the photo had turned out very nice.

He glanced down at her to make sure she was still smiling and she was looking up at him. "Things like this make me wish you were a different man."

He had no reply to that. He knew what she wanted to hear from him—words of commitment or at least a promise to move in that direction. But they were words he couldn't say. He'd made a promise to himself a long time ago that he'd never marry. That he'd never settle down because his father had said that Stern men weren't the kind that took too well to marriage.

And Nate had believed that after his broken engagement. So he'd steered clear of women like Jen. Women who could make him feel more than just fleeting pleasure and a sense of fun.

But somehow she'd snuck in, he thought. Last night she'd been a pretty girl that he wanted. Today she was starting to grow on him. Starting to make him want to make promises he knew he'd never be able to keep.

"Um…why don't you take some photos of the living quarters for Riley. I'm going to check the radar and get us ready to head back to shore."

She didn't say anything but turned and walked away. And he knew that was for the best. That the only way they were going to both be okay was if both of them walked away from each other now. He knew that a part of him would regret it but better to end things now before they had really even started than later when they'd both be hurt worse.

Seven

Nate drove her back to the club to get her car but she was reluctant to let the day end. He stood there in his chinos, deck shoes and T-shirt wearing a pair of Armani sunglasses and looking like temptation itself. Was it any wonder she didn't want him to leave?

"Want to have lunch with me? I don't have your stunning view at my place, but we do have a nice Florida room and I make the best grilled-cheese sandwiches in the world," she said. Standing next to her car with him made her feel more vulnerable than she would have guessed. But in the bright light of day, back in her real world, she knew how fleeting her time with Nate really was.

"World's best, eh? I can't pass that up."

"I'm glad. Do you want to follow me?"

"I have to stop at the office and check in with my

brothers. Give me your address and I'll meet you there in an hour."

She gave him the address, which he entered into his iPhone, and then he gave her his cell phone number and took hers. "So we can get in touch with each other if we need to."

He kissed her and then helped her into her car. She watched in the rearview mirror as she drove away. He stood there until she turned the corner.

She tried not to second-guess inviting him over. Marcia should be at the office and Riley usually had soccer in the afternoons.

But when she walked in the door, the first thing she heard was the sound of kids' voices and she knew that Riley was home.

"Aunt Jen. We won our game!" he said, running into the foyer to see her. "Lori brought us back here to have cupcakes and Coke."

"Great idea. Best way to celebrate," Jen said, even though that much sugar would make her nephew bounce off the walls.

Jen followed Riley down the hall into the kitchen where his nanny Lori and her son Edward were both sitting at the table. "I didn't know you were going to be home."

"It's okay. Do you need to head out? I can watch Riley until Marcia gets home."

"Actually, yes, I do."

"Then you can go if you need to," Jen said.

"Not yet, though," Riley said. "Edward and I are going to trade Silly Bandz."

"Go do that, but make it quick," Lori said.

"I thought you'd be home when I stopped by," Lori said once the boys were out of the room.

"I had a date," Jen said.

"A date? Good for you, girl. You spend too much time working and staying home."

Jen didn't know about that but she nodded. Edward and Riley ran back into the room before she had a chance to comment. The boys were busy chatting about the Bandz they'd exchanged.

"Come on, Edward, let's go."

Riley was disappointed to see his friend leave but got over it quickly. He was talking a mile a minute about the game and his game-winning goal. She listened to him and reminded herself that having her nephew in her life was one of the best things she experienced.

"What did you do today?" he asked.

She waggled her eyebrows at him. "I went out on a yacht."

"You did?"

"Yes. Want to see some pictures?"

"You bet," he said.

Jen showed him the photos she took and when she got to the one of her and Nate, Riley asked who he was.

"That's Nate. He's my friend that owns the yacht."

"Do you think I can go out on his boat?"

"I don't know, Riley, I will ask him."

"Thanks, Aunt Jen. Do you want to play Mario Kart?"

"Not right now," she said. "Why don't you have a game while I make some lunch? Nate is going to come over and join us."

Riley went into the living room and she soon heard the sounds of his Wii game powering up. She turned on the radio and looked around the kitchen. It was a nice area with a butcher-block island, stainless steel appliances and granite countertops. She'd moved in here when she'd first come back to Miami after being kicked off the competitive dancing tour.

Marcia had invited her to make this her home and together they had shaped this house up nicely. There was a photo of the three of them in Little Italy eating at Ferrara's bakery when they had visited New York last summer so Riley could see where his grandmother had grown up. The refrigerator was decorated with Riley's latest art projects and in the corner was a glass door that led out into the Florida room.

Beyond that was the backyard with a soccer net and a water feature that Jen had done herself after taking a Saturday morning class at the local hardware store.

She liked this place, but she'd never really intended it to be her home. She'd always assumed she'd be going back on tour and this place would be a base of operations.

But now, this might be it. And if it wasn't, she'd have to find her own place. Maybe something close by so she could still see Riley and her sister and help them out when they needed it.

She sat down at the breakfast bar realizing she had no idea what she wanted. This was a major crisis. The future was wide open and as of this moment, she had no idea what to fill it with.

She reached for the phone to call Nate and cancel, realizing that she didn't want him to come to this home. She didn't want to show him her life and see in his eyes that this wasn't what he wanted. Did she really need further proof that they weren't after the same things?

No, she knew she didn't need more evidence of that, but what she did need was to figure out what she wanted. And in the meantime, Nate was fun and a distraction.

As long as she remembered that she'd be okay and they could enjoy each other.

The radio started playing Gloria Estefan and the Miami Sound Machine's "Rhythm Is Gonna Get You" and she stood up to dance to it.

"Auntie! It's our song," Riley said, running into the kitchen. She laughed as he danced around her just as she'd taught him. They raised their hands over their heads and clapped to the beat as they both swiveled their hips to the music. They were laughing and clapping and dancing when the doorbell rang and she realized that dancing was still her life, just in a different way now.

Riley greeted Nate when the door opened. The sound of music floated down the hall and Jen stood behind her nephew laughing and swaying to the music. Nate paused there for a minute, seeing something that contradicted his personal experience of how women and sons got along. He knew that Jen wasn't the boy's mother but they were enjoying each other. He could see that from the expression on both of their faces.

"Hello, Mr. Nate," Riley said, holding out his hand for Nate to shake it.

Jen came up behind her nephew and put her arm around him as Nate shook his hand.

"Nice to meet you, Riley."

"Auntie and I were just dancing to 'our' song."

"What's your song?" Nate asked.

"'Rhythm Is Gonna Get You,'" Jen said. "Do you know it?"

"I do. It's a fun song," Nate said.

"Yes, it is. We danced all over the kitchen," Riley said. "Do you want to play the Wii while Auntie Jen finishes making lunch?" He glanced up at Jen.

"I know I enticed you over with grilled cheese. Is that still okay?"

Nate nodded. "Do you need my help?" he asked.

She shook her head. "I'll be about fifteen minutes."

She walked into the kitchen, which was off the main hall, as Riley led Nate into the living room. They had a plasma screen TV and a very comfy Italian leather sofa. Riley sat on the floor on a big pillow and offered Nate one that was tucked in the corner.

"I haven't played video games in a long time." This wasn't what Nate had expected. It was a little too domesticated for his tastes, and his instincts were screaming for him to run. Leave this house and go back to his real life.

"It's okay. I will go easy on you," Riley said.

Nate took the controller and played with the boy but his attention wasn't on the racetrack or the game. He glanced around the room.

This place was homier than his house. There were touches that showed a child lived there but you really got a sense of the women who called it home. On one wall were photos of Jen and her sister Marcia as girls and through their entire lives. He saw Jen in a skimpy Latin dancing costume holding a trophy. He saw Marcia standing on the steps of the courthouse holding her briefcase and grinning at the camera. And there was a photo of Jen holding her nephew in the hospital standing next to her sister's bed.

The two women were all each other had and their bond was just as deep and strong as the one he had with his brothers.

He knew women were caring so that didn't surprise him, it was just this was the first time he'd been involved with a woman who was like that. Even his own mother hadn't been a nurturer.

He sank deeper into the comfy couch and realized he could let himself get comfortable here. Not just in the house but in this life. But it wasn't his. He knew better than to try to pretend to be someone he wasn't.

"You lost," Riley said.

"I guess I did. Jen said you have a yellow-fin tuna in your room."

"Yes, I do," he said, hopping up. "We have to clean up before I show you. If I leave the controllers out I won't be able to play again for a week."

Nate nodded and helped Riley put the pillows back in a basket next to the entertainment center and the controllers away in the cabinet. Then Riley led the way to the stairs and up to his room.

The tuna was the dominant feature in the room. The bed was covered in a light blue comforter and there was a desk in one corner. Three toy boxes were lined up under the large plate-glass window. The walls were painted a sunny yellow color.

"I couldn't believe it when I caught that fish. I wasn't strong enough to land it by myself," Riley said. "Do you like fishing?"

"I do. I don't go often," Nate said. The last time he'd been was more than three months ago when Cam had insisted they all take a trip to St. Lucia.

"Why not?"

"Busy working."

Riley shook his head. "I don't understand why grownups work all the time. You finally don't have to go to school and instead of enjoying it…well, Mommy likes her job so that's why she does it. Is that how it is for you?"

"I guess it is. Do you think you'd enjoy working?"

"I know I'm going to," Riley said. "I'm going to be a fishing boat captain and spend all my time fishing."

"Sounds like a good plan," Nate said. When he'd been Riley's age he'd declared he was going to play baseball for a living so he knew that kids could make their dreams happen.

"Did you always want to be in business?" Riley asked.

"Nah, I used to play baseball."

"Really? I didn't know that. How come you don't play anymore?"

Nate wondered at kids and how they had no filter or fear. Riley wanted to know something so the kid just asked. "Let's head back downstairs and I'll tell you."

"Okay. Do you still play sometimes?"

"I don't play anymore, Riley. I got injured and had to change jobs."

Riley stopped on the stairs and looked back at him. "I'm sorry. I know I'd hate it if I couldn't fish."

Nate reached out and ruffled the kid's hair. "I can play now for fun, I just don't have the time because I'm always working."

"My best friend Edward's dad is like that. That's why he started coaching our soccer team. So he could play and relax…at least that's what Lori says."

"Who's Lori?"

"Edward's mom and my babysitter. Mommy and Auntie Jen can't be here all the time."

"Work?" Nate asked, getting the picture that the adults in Riley's life spent too much time working as far as the kid was concerned. He didn't want to care. This kid didn't matter to him if he was going to part ways with Jen. And he was going to leave her alone after this. Their lives were different and he wasn't willing to give up his lifestyle for her.

"Yes. But I know that they have to so I can have nice things and we can live in this house…don't say I was complaining about it, okay?"

Nate nodded just as Jen entered the foyer to call them to lunch. Riley was an interesting little kid and Nate liked what he learned about Jen from watching her with her nephew.

Nate had insisted they go to the local sports store and get a baseball bat, ball and gloves and go to the park and throw the ball with Riley. Riley was ecstatic and kept saying that Nate was obviously a man who knew life was about more than work.

Jen felt bad for her nephew because she and Marcia were gone more than they were home. But today made up for that.

Nate was patient as he talked Riley through how to throw a ball. "You are doing good."

"Your turn, Auntie Jen."

"I'm not as good at this as you are," Jen said. And then proved it by tossing the ball and completely missing Nate who stood with his glove ready to catch it.

Riley shook his head. "That was pitiful. Show her like you did me."

Nate walked over to her. "Get ready, Riley."

Nate walked over to her and stood behind her so close that she felt his body through the fabric of her clothing. He leaned in low.

"Bend your knees a little," he said.

She did what he instructed.

"Now, hold the ball like this," he said, showing her the proper way to hold the baseball.

He spoke directly into her ear sending chills down her spine and making this into so much more than just a kid's game in the park. He made her want to turn in his arms and kiss him. But Riley was waiting and hoping for some spectacular results.

"Next, bring your arm up like this. No, relax. Let me move your arm for you."

She did and the ball fell out of her hand on the ground. "Sorry."

"Its okay," he said, bending down to pick up the fallen ball and letting his hand stray to her hip where he caressed her as he stood back up. "Okay, ready?"

"I hope so. I'm a dancer not a baseball player," she said.

"I think today you will be both," Riley said.

"I will be," she said.

"Remember how I showed you to move your arm. Get ready, Riley."

"I'm ready, Nate. Come on, Auntie Jen, throw it to me."

Jen wound up and threw the ball. This time it went all the way to Riley who caught it and then whooped with joy. Nate put his arm around her waist and pulled her back against him for a quick kiss. "Great throw. You have the makings of a real player."

"I doubt that," she said.

Riley tossed the ball back and he and Nate played while she watched. Jen didn't want to risk messing up her record after that perfect throw. She had so much fun that she forgot that she was going to be cautious around Nate.

Her cell phone rang and she glanced at the ID to see that it was Marcia.

"Hey, there," Jen said by way of greeting.

"Hello. Where are you guys? Your car is here but you aren't."

"We are at the park playing catch."

"Catch? You stink at that."

"Ha, that's what you know. I'm much better today."

"Is Nate with you?"

"Yes, he came for lunch and then took Riley here to play."

"Really? That doesn't seem like the man I met last night," Marcia said.

"There's more to him than meets the eye," Jen said, watching Riley and Nate toss the ball back and forth. "We'll be home in a little while."

"Okay. Thanks for watching Riley this afternoon," Marcia said.

"I enjoy it. I love him."

"I know, but thanks all the same."

"It's no biggie," Jen said, hanging up the phone.

Nate led the way back over to her. "Was that your sister?"

"Yes. Mommy's home, Riley, you ready to go and see her?"

"Yes! I can't wait to show her how I can throw."

"I'm sure she will be very impressed," Jen said.

"Will you stay and throw with me, Mr. Nate? I don't think Auntie Jen will be a good partner for that," Riley said looking up at Nate.

"I'd love to, bud. I can't stay long, though. I've got a busy night ahead of me."

Riley tipped his head to the side. "Do you work at night?"

"That's when the club is open."

"You work with Auntie Jen?" he asked. "Are you a dancer?"

Nate laughed. "No. I own the club with my brothers."

Riley nodded. "Sounds like a good job."

Nate patted the little boy on the shoulder. "It's pretty good but there isn't enough time for baseball or fishing."

"But you are the boss," Riley said. "You should change the rules."

Jen laughed at the way Riley said it. That made perfect sense to him, but she'd love to see Nate tell Justin and Cam that they needed more time for fun. She was pretty sure those two would think he'd gone off the deep end since Nate's life was already one big party.

"I should do that," Nate agreed. When they got back to the house Nate walked them to the door.

Jen watched her nephew go inside, then turned to Nate. She couldn't read his expression but he'd kept his keys in his hand and had almost turned to walk back to his car. It was as if he couldn't wait to get away from here.

"Nate?"

"Hmm?"

"Thanks for everything you did with Riley today."

"No problem. I think he's the first kid I've been around since I was a child."

"My life is so different than yours," she said. But hadn't she truly known that from the beginning? They came from different worlds and that was part of why she liked him so much.

"Yes, it is. Well, I've got to go," he said.

"Bye."

She watched him walk away, realizing how good Nate was at making himself fit into whatever the situation was. Because it was only as he drove away that she realized he'd been the perfect uncle figure to Riley the way he'd been the perfect date to her last night.

She thought he was multifaceted but now she was afraid he was simply a chameleon used to changing his colors wherever he was. No matter how kind he was to Riley, Nate hadn't really wanted to spend time with her nephew and that, more than anything else, should serve as a reminder that he wasn't the settling-down kind.

Eight

"Hello, boys, thanks for taking time out of your busy schedules to meet with me," Cam said as he joined Justin and Nate in the VIP lounge at the back of the club on the first floor.

The place was empty except for staff as they had an hour before it opened.

"Not a problem. What's up?"

"We need to start working on the tenth anniversary celebration in May. Justin, I'd like you to reach out to the local community and try to get them involved in this. They are bringing in some big-shot lawyer from Manhattan to oppose overexpansion so if you can make sure they aren't up to anything that's going to cause us trouble, I'd appreciate it."

"I'm on it, big bro. There is a community open house tonight and I'm going to attend to see what's on everyone's mind."

"Good. Nate, I need you to pull out all the stops and get us some big-name A-listers for this thing. Not just people who will stop by, but celebs to headline the street party."

"I will hit the phone and see who I can get. What do you want them to do? Hutch will come and do a rap show I'm sure, but what else do you want?"

"I'm going to have Jen Miller choreograph a dance show that will run on Saturday night. I want to showcase everything the club has to offer."

"Okay, that's not a problem," Nate said. "I'll let you know in a few days who can make it. Are we still talking about Memorial Day weekend?"

"Yes," Cam said. "I am meeting with an event planner next week to approve invitations and coordinate our print media for the event. It's important that the Latin community feels a part of this. When you are at that event tonight, Justin, will you see if you can get some volunteers to help with this?"

"I will do that. I talked to our merchandise department and they are going to go ahead with the commemorative cigars. I got the final legal wrangling taken care of so we can use the old labels from this place along with our logo."

"That's going to be great," Cam said. "Boys, I can't believe we've been doing this ten years."

The rest of the meeting went by rather quickly and Nate found himself reluctant to leave. He wanted to talk to his brothers about their mom. For the first time in a long while he wanted to discuss her and figure out if his impressions and beliefs were the same as his brothers'.

Justin got up to go but Nate stopped him. "I...I went out on a date with Jen last night."

"Our employee?" Cam asked, his eyebrows furrowing in a way that Nate knew from his youth meant trouble.

"Yes. I didn't do anything inappropriate like threaten her job security, so chill out."

Cam stood up and leaned over the table. "Did you sleep with her?"

Nate didn't answer. Jen was private. What had happened with her wasn't for public consumption. "That's neither here nor there. I was letting you know because I might go out with her again."

He wanted to say she was different and see if his brothers had any clue as to why she would be the woman to make him react like this. But he would never ask them about that. He would never really be able to talk about her because that wasn't the kind of thing a man did.

"Good for you," Justin said. "I don't really know her, but if you are thinking of dating her, I say go for it."

Nate glanced at his middle brother. Justin looked the most like their mom out of the three of them. "Legally that's okay?"

"As long as you don't put her job on the line I think you're fine. I can draw up an agreement for you both to sign…"

Nate shook his head. "That doesn't sound good to me. Jen's different. She lives with her sister and her nephew."

Cam came around the table and sat down in the chair that Justin had vacated. "Family is important to her. She's not like the kind of girls you usually hang out with."

"I know that," Nate said. Cam was falling into big-brother mode. It didn't matter that he and Justin were adults now; Cam still felt that he had to watch over them and give them advice. "I can handle this."

Justin nodded. "He's a big boy."

Cam shook his head. "I don't care too much about that. I'm more concerned with the fact that I don't want to lose a valuable employee. She took my dream for the rooftop club and made it viable."

"You did that," Nate reminded his brother. "She's just talented enough to know how to get people up on their feet."

"Which is what makes this club so successful. Just play it cool, Nate. Don't let this get to be more than she can handle. I don't want to have to replace her."

Cam walked away before Nate could say anything else and he just watched him leave. Justin stood there for a second but Nate got up and left as well. He walked out of the club and started down Calle Ocho. He stood on the corner and looked back at Luna Azul.

He wasn't going to do anything to ruin the success he'd found here. He was too old to find another new career, especially since he really liked this one.

And he refused to be the man who stole this from Jen. She had a life here with Riley and her sister and he didn't want her to have to move on. He saw how much not being a competitive dancer had affected her and he knew she was putting her life back together piece by piece. The very last thing she needed right now was a man who was just looking for fun.

No matter that he wanted to be more than just a casual guy in her life, he knew he couldn't be. Because even though what he felt for her was intense, he knew it would burn out eventually and they'd both have to move on.

* * *

Jen woke Monday morning to the sounds of Riley and Marcia getting ready to leave. One of the nice things about her job was that she didn't have to rush out of bed every morning. She got up and put on her robe before going downstairs.

She hadn't heard from Nate yesterday but she knew that she wouldn't. They were both feeling their way through this thing—she was reluctant to call it a relationship because she wasn't sure she was ready for it yet.

"Morning, Auntie Jen," Riley said, giving her a hug.

"Morning, Riley."

"Mommy, I'm ready."

"Great. I need to talk to Auntie Jen. You head out to the car."

Riley nodded and went out the front door. Marcia stood in the doorway so she could remotely unlock the car and keep an eye on Riley.

"I left the newspaper out for you."

Jen glanced at her sister. "I don't read it."

"You'll want to this morning. There's a picture of Nate in it with some woman—a Spanish royal or something."

Jen nodded. She'd just said they weren't dating so why would this news hurt. "It's fine. We're just friends."

Marcia reached out and hugged her. "I can come back after I drop Riley off if you want to talk. I'm not due in court today."

"No, don't do that. I have a meeting at eleven at the club to talk about the tenth anniversary celebration. Besides, it was just one date."

Jen didn't want to talk about this. She wanted to hide

away until she figured out why she felt so hurt. She knew he wasn't the kind of man who was going to give up his jet-set lifestyle for her after one date.

"I'll be fine. Have a good day."

Marcia pursed her lips. "I know you'll be fine. But that doesn't mean this won't hurt. You didn't need this now."

"Marcia, stop. I'm trying to get it under control in my head. Don't make me hash it out or I'll start crying."

Her sister hugged her again and then turned to leave. "Call me if you need me."

"I will."

Jen closed the door on her sister and nephew and leaned back against it. She didn't want to go and look at a picture of Nate with another woman. Especially since she'd dreamed about his arms around her all night. She'd dreamed of them being on that yacht of his together and making love on the sundeck.

She put her hands in her hair and stood there for a minute trying to get her head around the idea. It didn't matter that she'd already thought he might not be serious about her. She didn't want to see the proof that the very next night he'd gone out with someone else.

But she wasn't a coward and she never ran away from anything. She walked into the kitchen and saw the coffee mug her sister had left for her next to the paper. There was a Post-it note on it in Marcia's handwriting warning her that there was a picture of Nate inside.

She poured herself a cup of coffee and then took the mug and the paper outside with her. She sat down on the bench next to the water feature and let the scents of the garden surround her. The sweet smell of jasmine mingled with the scent of hibiscus in the air. The sound of the water flowing in the fountain soothed her troubled nerves.

She took a sip of her coffee and then set it on the ground at her feet before she opened the paper. The *Miami Herald* didn't have anything as lurid and gossipy as the New York papers but they did have a society page owing to how many celebrities made South Florida their home.

The picture was…she looked away and then made herself look back at it. Nate had his arm around the other woman and she was laughing and looking up at him. The same way that Jen had looked up at him. She'd been pressed to his side and she knew the weight of his arm on her shoulder…knew how it felt to be that close to him. And this hurt.

She tossed the paper aside and picked up her coffee mug. She walked around the garden wondering what to do. Alison had said that men who were fun liked to have fun. And that the only way to be successful in that kind of dating situation was to realize it was all about fun.

But to be honest, Jen had no idea how to do that. She wasn't a fun girl. She wanted it to mean something that she'd had sex with him. And that they'd talked about their pasts. She needed it to mean more than just a bit of fun.

And that wasn't Nate's fault. It was her burden. She was the one who'd been impulsive and jumped before seeing where she'd fall.

This was what her sister had tried to warn her about. But there was no way that she could have heeded that advice. There was something seductive about Nate. It wasn't just the sex, though, that had been earth-shattering. It was more the man behind the image.

If he'd just been the charming playboy then she'd

have expected this, but he'd seemed to be more than that. Now she was going to have to deal with the fact that he'd moved on. That was what he did.

She took another sip of her coffee. She couldn't hide away here or even quit and try to find another job. There weren't that many high-level clubs that needed Latin dancers. She just wasn't going to find another job like this and she didn't want to leave her home again.

She'd had a lot of time to think yesterday while she'd been watching Riley and it had occurred to her that not getting back on the dance circuit had been a good thing. It was time for her to start settling down and thinking about family.

Forget that at the time she'd spun silly fantasies in her head of Nate giving up his playboy lifestyle and settling down with her. The truth that she'd discovered yesterday still remained. She was ready to start looking for a home. To start making a life for herself.

And she didn't want to have to start again somewhere where she had no roots, no family and no friends. She refused to let Nate Stern drive her away from the job and the community that she'd started making her own. She'd just stay away from him and he'd never know how much that one night of fun had cost her.

Nate had reached for his phone to call Jen but stopped himself. If he'd come to any conclusions after meeting with his brothers, it was that he needed to break things off with her. And he had in the only way he knew. He'd moved on.

Countess Anika de Cuaron y Bautista de la Cruz was the sister of one of Nate's oldest friends, the Spanish Count Guillermo. Gui and some friends owned a string of European nightclubs called Seconds. So taking his sister out for the night was the least that Nate could do. They were like family.

And last night that had been the best that Nate could do. Somehow none of the other women he'd been dating casually had seemed right. There was only one woman he wanted to spend the night with and it was Jen.

But he wasn't the right kind of man for her. She deserved someone who could give her more than he could.

So here he was at a meeting where he didn't want to be trying to figure out why she wasn't looking at him. They were seated in the executive boardroom at the club's downtown Miami offices. Justin sat at one end of the table with his assistant, head chef Antonio Caruso sat next to him and head of security Billy Pallson was next to him.

Jen had taken a seat two down from Billy on the opposite side of the table from Nate. Nate had enough "relationship" skills to know that she was pissed off at him. Though that was what he'd anticipated when he'd gone out with Anika and made sure that their photo had hit all the papers—local, national and international—he still didn't like it.

"Let's get this meeting started," Cam said as he entered the room. His executive assistant, Tess, followed him along with another woman who Nate didn't know.

"This is Emma Nelson, the event planner I've hired to help us organize the party," Cam said. He then introduced everyone at the table before giving Emma the floor.

She handed out action item lists for each venue and it wasn't long before Nate realized that he wasn't paying attention to anything except Jen. He watched as she took notes, watched as she took a sip of her water and then looked away when she glared over at him.

He didn't understand it but it seemed that he wasn't ready to be done with Jen. Hell, he'd known that last night when he'd gone out with Anika but that didn't mean he could change it.

But Jen deserved a chance to have her dreams and he wasn't the kind of guy who could give them to her. He'd seen that at her home when she'd danced with her nephew, and in the park when she'd played baseball with him. He'd noticed the way her gaze lingered on him as he'd played with Riley. He'd have had to be a fool not to have been aware of the sexual tension there just beneath the surface when he'd taught her to throw.

Hell, right now he wanted her. If he had his way he'd tell everyone to leave and make love to her on this boardroom table. Jen wasn't the kind of woman who elicited a soft reaction from him. She called to him. Called to the passion inside of him and he wanted to answer that call but he knew that it would mean taking a chance on caring for her.

Caring for her? Since when had he become someone who talked to himself in euphemisms? His entire life he'd never let anything stand in the way of what he wanted.

Glancing across the table at Jen, seeing the way the sun brought out some blonde highlights in her dark hair, reminded him of how she'd looked out on his yacht.

He wanted to see her there again. He didn't want to back off because Cam had made him think that Jen wanted more from life than he could give. He wasn't the kind of man who gave up what he wanted and he wasn't going to give up Jen.

No way.

"Nate?"

"Yes?"

"Emma asked who we have booked on the main stage," Cam said.

"Hutch Damien. He will be doing his rap show and I think he'll want to coordinate with Jen and her dancers to use them on the stage as well. Jen and I can meet later to discuss that."

Hutch would be a big draw. He had been compared to Will Smith, and for the anniversary bash, Nate had asked him to include some Latin beats in the background.

"Good," Cam said. "Who else?"

"Ty Bolson and his wife, Janna McGree, will come and do a concert as well. They have a huge country music fan base. I'm not sure how you want to coordinate that. I've also asked my former teammates from the Yankees to come and hold a pitch competition."

"Sounds great," Emma said. "I think since the focus is on Luna Azul we should have the concerts in the club. But maybe have them do one or two songs outside. I can set up a stage on the street if you think we can get the community to agree to letting us have the block party."

"Justin was working on that," Cam said.

"I attended a meeting last night of comunity leaders and I have another meeting set up today to try to talk to them. Right now they are reluctant to agree to anything. They have filed an injunction to keep the marketplace we've acquired from being rebuilt. I'll be meeting with their lawyer to discuss the details."

"Thank you, Justin," Cam said. "Billy, as far as security goes, what do you recommend? We want this to be a free event but not a free-for-all."

"I have my guys set up a perimeter so that we cover

the entire area outside the club. Inside, I'll have our usual coverage and a few extra teams."

Cam nodded. "Emma, will you need to meet with Billy to discuss this?"

"I will need to meet with everyone one-on-one to discuss the details. We have a lot to do," Emma said.

The meeting started to wind down and Nate saw Jen gathering all of her notes. He had a feeling she was going to make a fast break for it.

"Jen, do you have time to stay and meet with me about the show?" Nate asked. "My office is just down the hall."

She looked up at him and then she nodded.

"Sounds good," Cam said. "I want everyone back here this time next week. We will be meeting weekly until the party. Thank you."

Everyone left and Jen stood there in the boardroom waiting for him. "I don't know where your office is."

"I know. I will show you the way."

He led her to his office at the end of the hall. His secretary offered them drinks but Jen declined, and then they entered his office and he closed the door behind them.

"You are very good at that."

"What do you mean?" he asked.

"That you know how to show a girl a good time, and that's all."

Nine

Jen should have known that she'd run into Nate. Should have figured that just because she'd decided to avoid him that it wouldn't happen. Should have known that she'd still want him as soon as she saw him.

It didn't help matters that he looked so good today. His shirt was left open at the collar revealing his tanned neck. His pants were fashionable and fit him perfectly. The fact that he kept looking at her wasn't helping either. Because in his eyes she saw things she thought she wanted to see. She thought she saw regret and a desire to give things a try.

But she knew she was fooling herself. That was just her imagination going crazy. Hadn't she already learned her lesson when her relationship with Carlos had taken dance away from her?

Was she going to be one of those women who never made smart choices when it came to men?

"Thank you for agreeing to meet with me now," he said.

"Did I have a choice?" she asked.

He raised an eyebrow at her. "Yes, you did."

"I know. I'm just out of sorts today. Tell me what kind of dancing you think we'll need for Hutch's set. I've only heard a couple of his songs on the radio so I'm not as familiar with him as I should be. Do you think we can get him to come down and rehearse with us?"

"I don't want to talk business first. I want to sort out this business between us."

"What business? We went out on a date and 'hooked up.' That was it."

Nate shook his head. "We didn't hook up. Things between us aren't that casual and you're not that kind of girl."

"It doesn't matter, you are that kind of man."

"I guess you saw the photo of me and Anika?"

"Yes, I did. I knew you weren't the relationship kind, Nate. So that photo didn't tell me anything I didn't already know."

Nate walked over to the window and looked out at the city. He wasn't sure what he was really looking for, just knew that he didn't want to face Jen anymore. She had made a statement of fact and her words shouldn't bother him but they did.

"I don't want you to think that you mean nothing to me."

"I don't. I think we both weren't ourselves and that's why we were able to connect. But I...I don't want to let you drive me away from this place. It's my home and since I'm starting over, this is the best job for me to do that."

Nate turned to face her. "I get that. I realized while

we were in the meeting today that I want more from you than I thought I did. Actually, that's not true. I knew it from the beginning but I was afraid you'd turn out not to be the woman I thought you were."

She nibbled on her lower lip, something he knew she did when she was nervous. "Who do you think I am?"

"Someone who cares deeply about the people she surrounds herself with. I know that my connections and my friends aren't the reason why you were with me the other night. And that is something I'm not used to."

"I get that, Nate. I'm not sure what you want from me," she said.

"I want a chance to date you. To get to know you and see if there's anything between us besides sex."

She nodded. "That's honest."

"Yes, it is. I'm not going to lie to you, Jen. Not about anything. There are going to be times when I have to go out with different women and I'm going to have to get my photo in the papers but that's publicity and that's for the club. That's not about you and me. Can you handle that?"

She tipped her head to the side studying him and he hoped she'd find what she was looking for when she looked at him.

"I might be able to. I can handle you working with women but I don't want to be made a fool of. If we're going out I need you to be monogamous with me. I'm not willing to settle for being part of your harem."

That startled a laugh out of him. "I don't have a harem. Never have wanted one, either. I just want to have fun. And I think you and I can enjoy the hell out of life together."

"I can handle that," she said. "I'm not in a place to

get serious either, but I like you and to be honest, I'm not ready to move on."

He came around his desk. "Good. Let's seal the deal with a kiss."

"The deal? This isn't a business arrangement."

"I know. Hence the kiss," he said.

She smiled at him and it was the first time today that he'd seen her seem happy. He was glad he'd talked to her. Glad he'd decided to go after Jen. She was the kind of woman that he'd regret not knowing if he let her slip away now.

She walked over to him and kissed him softly on the lips. He put his arms around her and drew her close. Holding her made him realize that he'd feared he'd never get to hold her again.

He tightened his arms around her and then realized what he was doing. He didn't want her to know how much she meant to him. Even now when they'd only really had one date—but what a date. He'd wanted their time together to never end.

He had to find a way to bind her to him. To keep her close to him without giving up any more of his emotions. Because caring for Jen would be his downfall if he didn't handle it the right way.

Jen had thought she'd never feel his arms around her again and she was so glad that she was back here now. She rested her head on his chest right over his heart and heard the strong beating of it under her ear.

He skimmed his hands up and down her back before settling them on her hips. She felt his erection stir, nudging her at her center. She looked up at him as he lowered his head to kiss her.

His lips rubbed over hers and then his tongue traced

the seam of her lips. She parted them and invited his tongue to come deeper into her mouth, which it did.

His tongue tasted her in long languid strokes and she forgot everything. She was back in his arms, the one place she'd dreamed of being since he'd last left her on her doorstep.

He leaned back against his desk and pulled her against him. His hands continued to skim her body and she found she couldn't get enough of touching him. She wanted more. She wanted his clothing out of her way so she could feel his flesh against hers.

She reached between their bodies, stroking him through his pants. She ran her finger down the zipper and then reached between his legs to cup him.

He widened his stance so she could keep her hand where it was. She played with him with one hand and then brought the other down to slowly lower his zipper. She felt the fabric of her skirt being drawn slowly up her legs and then Nate's hands were on her buttocks. She felt him stroking her through the thin material of her panties.

Once she had his zipper lowered she reached into his pants to stroke his rock-hard length. He grew even harder under her touch. He turned and lifted her up onto his desk. His pencil jar spilled and the noise was startling, when she pulled back from kissing him, she looked up into his eyes.

His pupils were dilated with desire. His skin was flushed and his body was aggressive in trying to assuage his needs. His hips thrust between her thighs, his hands working to draw the fabric of her blouse up her body.

She felt his hands against her stomach and then higher as he palmed her breasts.

She reached lower and finished undoing his pants,

freeing him from his underwear. He was thick and hot under her hand and as she stroked him, he whispered in her ear.

Telling her how much he wanted her. How much he couldn't wait to be buried deep in her soft warm body. And then she felt him between her legs. One arm wrapped around her waist, he lifted her up as he pulled her panties away from her body. He got them as far as her thighs before he had to step back.

In an impatient move, he shoved them down her legs and then put his hands on her thighs and spread her legs wide. "Are you ready for me?"

"Once you get a condom."

She nodded and reached for him, drawing him closer to her. He stepped back between her legs. Bracing his hands on the desk beside her hips, he probed at her opening with the tip of his manhood. She was wet and ready. Desperate to be one with him again.

And this time he plunged deep into her. Took her like he meant to make her his completely. He thrust deeply into her again and again until everything in her body seemed to focus on that point of contact. She felt herself getting closer and closer to the edge until she went over. She opened her mouth to say his name but he kissed her and captured the sound.

He thrust into her two more times before he came, his hips jerking forward as he filled her with his essence. She was breathing like she'd run a race—she felt as if she just had. She wrapped her arms around his chest and rested her head on his shoulder.

She took comfort from having him here with her. She knew that she hadn't been ready to move on and no matter what she'd said to him, Nate was important to her.

"That was one hell of a kiss," he said.

She smiled up at him. "You go to my head."

"Good," he said, he pulled slowly out of her body and reached around her for a box of tissues. He handed her a couple and then cleaned himself off. "I have a washroom through that door if you want to clean up."

She hopped off his desk and bent to pick up her panties. "With any other man I might be embarrassed now."

"But not with me?"

She shook her head. "Everything always feels natural with you."

He nodded. "I'm glad to hear that."

She went into the washroom and used the hand towel to clean up. Her hair was tousled and her lips were swollen. Even though she righted her clothing, it wouldn't take a detective to figure out what they'd been up to in his office.

But she didn't care. He said that they were going to try to date each other and she wasn't going to be embarrassed by anything that happened between them.

Nate was the kind of man who lived life with passion. For a long time she'd channeled all of her energy into dancing. It was about time she got out of the rehearsal hall and into the real world. Nate was the perfect man to share this with.

She tried to caution herself as she looked in the mirror not to get in over her head but she knew it was too late. It had been too late since the first time she'd danced with him.

Nate was different and she cared about him. That was why that photo had hurt so much this morning. Why sitting across the boardroom table had been such agony and why she'd agree to just about anything if it meant she'd see him again.

She opened the door to rejoin him and he told her he'd be a minute in the washroom. She walked over to the plate-glass windows and glanced out at his view. The city sprawled as far as the eye could see.

"You okay?" he asked when he rejoined her a few minutes later.

"I am. I feel a lot better about everything."

"I'm glad. Now what do you say we talk business."

"Sounds good."

She had no idea what the future held for them but she was sure that she wasn't going to be just existing and that made her feel really good about her life post-dancing.

The next few weeks flew by as he balanced his new life. He had no regrets about dating Jen. It was turning out to be one of the best decisions of his life. He was finding that he didn't need to actually date famous women to get their photos in the paper. In fact, the more he included different groups of his famous friends in the club's events, the more he found that some of them had settled down. And that most of them didn't miss their old single days.

It was an eye opener for him. He was happy just being with Jen but thoughts of the future made him a little edgy.

For one, he wasn't too sure about the details of her past and why she left the competitive dancing world behind.

So when Carlos Antonio showed up at Luna Azul and demanded to see Jen one Friday afternoon, Nate felt like he was closer to finding the truth she'd been keeping to herself.

"She's in a class right now," Nate said as they stood in the VIP ticket area under the Chihuly glass ceiling.

"I will wait," Carlos said. Carlos wasn't very tall and he was slim. He was well-dressed and appeared to be in his early forties.

"Let's go up to the rooftop club. Jen will be leading the class out there to help open the dance floor."

"Who are you?"

"Nate Stern, I co-own the club with my brothers. And you are Carlos Antonio, correct?"

"Yes, I am the world-famous dancer."

Nate rolled his eyes. This guy was a pompous ass from what he could tell. He'd been hassling the girls at the ticket booth for almost forty-five minutes before they'd paged him to come and take care of this guy.

"That's where you know our Jen from, then," Nate said.

"Indeed, it is. Have you heard of me?"

Nate shook his head. "I don't follow ballroom dancing. I'm more into sports."

He saw the other man flinch. Keeping in mind that this man was probably a friend of Jen's, Nate thought he should stop needling him. "Sorry about that. I know little of the world of dance."

"Most people don't," Carlos said. "I will go with you to wait for Jen."

Nate led the way to the rooftop club and found a seat for them both. "What can I get you to drink?"

"Jack Daniels on ice."

Nate signaled the waitress and placed the order. "Do you live here?"

"No. I'm here for a competition and thought I'd stop by and see Jen."

Nate wasn't getting much from this guy. He was glad

when the music turned to the familiar "Mambo No. 5" and he saw Jen and her students come out on the dance floor.

She glanced over at him but when she saw who was sitting next to him she lost her ready smile. And her rhythm as the song began. But then she found it again and led the class.

Nate glanced over at Carlos who was sitting back in his chair looking self-satisfied. Nate had the feeling that Carlos had wanted to rattle Jen and that he was pleased that he had.

Nate's first instinct was to reach over and punch the guy. But he restrained himself.

"Why are you here?" Nate asked.

"I told you to see Jen. We have unfinished business," Carlos said.

"I don't think you do. I know for a fact that Jen has left that world behind."

"Do you? Or did it perhaps leave her behind?" Carlos asked.

"Either way she's out of it now," Nate said. He wondered if Carlos was an old partner of hers come to gloat over the fact that he could still dance while she was out of that world. Nate knew men like that. Had encountered more than one player who had treated him that way after he'd been forced to retire.

"I think you should leave," Nate said.

"I'm staying until I talk to her," Carlos said. "You can leave me here if you want to."

Nate did just that. He walked over to the stage and waited for Jen to finish leading the class. He knew she had to go backstage and change into her flamenco costume for the show with Alison in a short while, but this wasn't something that could wait.

When the lesson was over, she rushed into the dressing room before he could catch her. But as soon as she came out, he cornered her.

"Who is Carlos and what does he mean to you?" Nate asked as soon as they were alone.

"He was…I can't go into this now. There's not enough time to explain. Suffice it to say that he's the reason I'm not dancing anymore."

"I will have security throw him out," Nate said.

He turned to go get Billy, but Jen stopped him with her hand on his arm. "Wait. I want to hear what he has to say. Maybe he knows a way to convince the appeal board to consider my request one more time."

Nate didn't like it. He didn't like the fact that Carlos might be able to help her or that she might want to return to the world of competitive dance. "I thought you were happy with the life you are building here."

"I am. I just want to hear what he has to say."

"Okay. Let me know if you need me. I'm going down to the main club."

"Nate, it's nothing to worry about. I'm not going to change my mind. I just need to know why he's here."

He nodded. "I can respect that. Send me a text when he's gone and I'll come and join you."

"I will," she said. Then she leaned up and kissed him, and he let that quick embrace soothe the savage part of him.

The part that wanted to go back to that table and lift the world-famous dancer up by his lapels and tell him that Jen was his now. And this was his world and he wasn't welcome in it.

Ten

Once their dance routine was over, Jen changed out of her flamenco costume and bade goodbye to Alison. She was anxious to see why Carlos was here. She hoped he'd finally stopped saying she'd slept with him to ensure a better score if he were to judge one of her competitions. She wanted him to admit that their affair had started out of their friendship. She wasn't sure she'd return to the world of dance competitions but she would like to have her name cleared.

And he was the only man who could do it. Carlos had gotten word that their affair was common knowledge and gone to the other judges behind her back. Telling them that his guilt wouldn't let him continue to sleep with her. Though he hadn't judged her in an actual competition, the appearance of impropriety was there. The damage was already done.

Being demoted from the world stage to a regional

judge had punished him for their fraternization, but he had been able to stay in the competitive dance world, something that she hadn't. Why was he back now?

She knew that Nate wasn't too happy that she wanted to talk to Carlos and she wondered what he'd think if he knew that she and Carlos had been lovers. That was something she didn't want to find out. Things were going well between her and Nate and she didn't want to rock the boat.

She forced herself to take her time instead of racing back out to the table where Carlos waited for her. She pulled her hair up into a loose chignon and fixed her makeup. She wore a pair of skinny jeans, strappy sandals and a blousy top that tied on the side of her waist. Nate had promised to take her on a midnight cruise of Biscayne Bay and she was looking forward to that. If Carlos had good news, she'd be able to tell Nate more about her past.

She entered the club and saw Carlos sitting by himself watching the room. She wondered sometimes what she'd seen in him as a man. She had long suspected that her infatuation with him stemmed solely from the dance. They'd taught kids together as part of an outreach program when they'd been on tour and Carlos had been a different man on the dance floor. He'd been a special guest judge because of his reputation in the dance world.

He stood up when he saw her approaching and she smiled at him. "Good evening, Carlos. It is such a surprise to see you here."

"Good evening, Jen."

He sat back down and she did the same.

"Why are you here?" she asked.

"The competition is in town."

"But you aren't judging in it," she said.

"Very true. I heard that you'd appealed to the board again to reinstate you."

"Yes, I have. I want to have my name cleared."

"I need you to let this drop," Carlos said.

"Why? You didn't lose anything. I did. I want my name back."

"You're not going to get it," Carlos said. "You should stop trying to make that happen."

"You are probably right. So why are you really here?"

"I need your help," he said.

"What?"

"You heard me."

"Why would I help you?" she asked.

"You owe me."

She didn't even want to imagine how it was he thought she owed him. "What exactly do you need?"

"A recommendation as a dance instructor at the Calle Ocho School."

"Why me?"

"Your bosses own the marketplace where the dance studio is. So use your connections and I will get out of your hair."

"Will you tell the board what really happened between us?"

"Let that go," he said. "You can't go back. Holding on to the past is keeping you from moving on."

That wasn't true. She'd moved on. But she still wanted to clear her name. "I'll see what I can do, but I don't know if I will be able to help you out."

"I can make things rough for you, Jen. Tell Nate why you had to leave dancing before."

She shook her head. "He doesn't care about what happened in the world of dance."

"Just do this for me, Jen. And I'll be out of your hair."

She doubted it. Seeing Carlos again reminded her that she'd been stupid once when it came to men, and she didn't want to make the same mistake twice.

"I'll see."

"Make sure you do it. You know that Luna Azul is having trouble with the local business leaders and I'm not afraid to use my friends in this neighborhood to make their business dealings even more complex."

She did know that. But she thought it was ridiculous that Carlos was threatening her. She could quit if it really would hurt Luna Azul.

"I'll do what I can."

"You'll do what I ask or I will make life really uncomfortable for you. If I don't get this job…"

"What? I can't guarantee you a position, Carlos."

"You better hope you can. If not, it's going to take a lot of money to keep me quiet."

He got up and left the table. She sat there watching him, wondering how she'd ever let herself get involved with someone like that. He had no morals at all and was a complete jerk.

But that didn't mean she was going to be able to ignore him. She knew she had to let not only Nate but also Cam, who was her immediate boss, know what Carlos had threatened.

Her phone vibrated in her pocket and she glanced down at the ID screen to see a text from Nate. He wanted to know if she was okay.

She swallowed hard and knew that the mistakes of her past were going to be a very real threat in a few minutes. She didn't relish the idea of telling Nate about Carlos but she really had no choice.

She sent him a text saying that Carlos had left and she'd come and find him in the club.

"No need," he said, coming up behind her. "I'm here. Are you really okay? You look pale."

"I…can we go someplace and talk?"

"Sure. Why?"

"Because a club isn't the place to discuss this."

"What happened? Annie told me that it looked like you were fighting with Carlos."

One of the club waitresses spied for Nate?

"How did Annie get in touch with you?" Jen asked.

"I asked her to keep an eye on you and let me know if you got in trouble."

"Nice. Don't you trust me?" she asked, feeling bruised by her encounter with Carlos. She needed Nate to just accept her the way she was and back her up.

"You, I trust. That Carlos guy, not so much. What did he want?"

"I can't talk about it here," she said.

"Then let's go," he said.

She'd expected him to lead her to the backstage area where they'd talked the first night but instead he hustled her downstairs and out to his car. "Let's drive to the beach and you can tell me what's going on."

"Sounds good," she said. She needed time to figure out what she was going to say and how she was going to tell him that her past was threatening his future.

"Do you want to tell me while we are driving?" he asked.

"No. I need to think about this."

"Is it bad?"

"I don't know yet, but then Carlos has always been bad news."

"Carlos is a little jerk, Jen. And I don't mind showing that little dancer boy that you are with a real man now."

She shook her head. This was going to be a lot more complicated than she'd hoped.

As Nate walked down the beach with Jen, he reached out and took her hand in his. He hoped she knew that he was on her side. He wanted her to understand that he wasn't going to stand by and let anyone threaten her. Nate hadn't liked Carlos from the moment he'd met him and that was saying something.

"What did Carlos want?"

"A job and money, I think. Though he didn't tell me an amount," she said, tucking a strand of hair behind her ear.

That was the last thing he'd expected. He thought he might have to worry about Carlos talking her back into the world of competitive dance. He saw how good she was at dancing and he wasn't clear why she'd left.

"Okay, let's break this down. What job?"

"One at a dance school in the marketplace that you guys bought."

"We're not going to influence anyone to hire him."

"If you don't, he's going to use my past to bribe me into paying him."

"Why would he want money?" he asked, not following.

She nibbled her lower lip and then looked away from him. "There is no easy way to say this, Nate. I made a very stupid decision several years ago and had an affair with him when he was a judge for the World Competitive

Dance Federation. That's why I got kicked off the tour and banned from competition."

"What?"

She wrapped her arms around her waist and spoke so softly he had to lean forward to hear her.

"I know it was a stupid thing to do but I never asked him to cheat or do anything like that. We seemed to have a lot in common and I thought we were friends."

Nate drew her closer to him. He didn't like what he was hearing. "You had an affair with Carlos?"

"Yes. Tonight I had hoped he was here to help me clear my name. Remember, I told you the night we met that the board had denied my last appeal. But Carlos didn't come to help me."

Nate put his arm around her shoulders and pulled her close. "Instead, he wants money from you or what?"

"He said that the local leaders are already angry with the club and that if we don't help him, his word will be all it takes to ruin your business dealings."

Nate was angry. Carlos was an idiot if he thought he could intimidate one of the Luna Azul employees. It didn't matter that he himself was involved with Jen; the Stern brothers would stand by any of their employees, as long as they hadn't broken the law.

"Okay, here is what we are going to do. Justin is not only a financial wizard but he is also a lawyer—our corporate lawyer—and he's very good at what he does. I'm going to call him and we are going to figure out how to stop Carlos."

Jen pulled back. "I don't want everyone to know that I had an affair with him."

"I don't see why anyone has to know that besides Justin. He's smart about these kinds of things," Nate said, remembering that Justin had helped Cam with a false paternity suit years ago. "Let me talk to him and we'll figure this out. You aren't helping Carlos or paying him a single dime and we are going to get your good name back."

"I don't want to hurt the club," she said.

"You won't," he assured her. "When are you supposed to help him?"

"I don't know. I'm supposed to meet him at the Hallandale dance competition and let him know my decision."

That didn't leave a lot of time. "We need to meet with Justin as soon as possible and get his thoughts on this. Frankly, the only solution I can think of is beating the crap out of Carlos. It would make me feel better but I doubt it would help the situation."

She smiled at him. "You'd beat him up for me?"

"Sure would. I don't like guys who threaten women."

She leaned up and kissed him. "Thank you. That's one of the sweetest things anyone has ever offered to do for me."

"Not a problem, honey," Nate said. He wasn't kidding about hurting Carlos. Normally, Nate wasn't a violent man but to think of someone who'd been intimate with Jen and betrayed her then come back into her life to twist the knife…well, it made him livid. "I'm going to give Justin a call."

She nodded. "If you think that's the best idea, then okay."

"I think it's the only solution. Blackmailers are only successful when someone is willing to pay them. We need to stop this now before it gets out of control."

"I agree. I want him out of my life forever. I am so tired of him screwing me."

"We're going to take care of it," Nate said.

He called Justin's cell and his brother answered on the first ring. "We need to talk."

"Now?" Justin asked.

"Yes. Jen just received a blackmail threat and I want it eliminated."

"What are the circumstances?" Justin asked.

"Can you come to my yacht and we can talk there?" Nate asked. He thought they needed to get the details hammered out tonight.

"I can. Give me about forty-five minutes to get there."

"That's fine. I've got Jen with me. Thanks, Justin," Nate said.

"Do you want me to call Cam or are you going to?" Justin asked.

"I'll call him," Nate said. "See you later."

He hung up and turned to Jen. "Justin is going to meet us in forty-five minutes at the yacht."

"Who else do you have to call?"

"Cam," Nate said.

"They are going to think the worst of me," Jen said. "I know that what I did—"

"No one is going to judge you. He's blackmailing you and threatening the club. It has nothing to do with what you did when you were dancing," Nate said.

"I'm so sorry I ever got involved with Carlos," Jen said. "He has cost me so much. I really don't want to have to leave Luna Azul, but if you think it's best I will do it."

"You aren't leaving the club," Nate said. "I'm going to make this right."

"It's not your fault."

"No, nor is it yours. You made a bad choice but it led you to my door. I'm not going to let it be something you regret."

Jen tried to relax while they waited for Cam to appear. Nate had given her a glass of pinot grigio and she sat on the yacht deck under the stars, listening to the faint sound of Nate and Justin talking. Soon they rejoined her, taking a seat next to her on the bench.

"Tell me everything from the beginning," Justin said.

"Well, when I came out to the rooftop club Carlos was sitting with Nate," Jen said, thinking that was the best place to start.

"No. Tell me what happened with Carlos and why he thinks he can use that to blackmail you."

"Should we wait for Cam? I don't want to have to tell this too many times," she said.

"No, Cam will just want to know what our course of action is," Justin said.

Nate slid closer to her and took her hand in his. Feeling his support made her heart swell and she knew she was falling for him.

"Carlos and I had an affair while I was dancing on the tour and he was a judge. I was careful to never talk to him about the competition," she said. "And he never actually scored an event I competed in."

"How did the affair start then?" Justin asked.

"Does that matter?" Nate asked.

"Why don't you go and call Cam? See what's keeping him," Justin said.

"No. I'll keep my mouth shut. Just don't badger her," Nate said.

"I'm not," Justin said. "So?"

"We met at a kids' dance class. The tour sponsors dance workshops at each city we go to in order to introduce competitive ballroom to kids. He and I were partnered in a five-city gig. After the first day, he invited me to dinner and we just had a lot in common."

"How long did the affair last?"

"Just those three weeks," she said. "As soon as I went into the ballroom after sleeping with him, it felt wrong. I told him it didn't feel right and the next week he revealed to the judging board that we'd slept together and that I had seduced him to help improve my scores."

"What did the board do?"

"Suspended both of us. Carlos was demoted to a regional judge. I thought we could work together for an appeal and approached him to ask him to recant what he said and just talk to the board on my behalf...I thought that was why he'd come to the club tonight."

"But that wasn't the case," Nate said. "He wants help from her."

"Let her tell me," Justin said. "What does he want from you?"

"He didn't say. Actually I'm supposed to meet him in two days' time to tell him my decision. He really wants a job with the dance school in the marketplace you guys own. He's hoping I can influence the decision. He implied that if I don't help him, he'd come after us for money."

"What did he threaten?" Justin asked.

"To hurt the club's standing in the neighborhood. If I don't help or pay him he's going to stir up a lot of bad publicity."

"Okay," Justin said. "Let me think about this. Did anyone else know about your affair?"

"My partner Ivan."

"Did he see the two of you together?" Justin asked.

"He had dinner with us when Carlos asked me out."

"Why didn't you ask him to vouch for you?" Justin asked.

"I did. He wrote a letter but they said since he was my partner, they couldn't count on him telling the truth," Jen said. "Ivan was pretty upset because my being suspended effectively shut him out as well. That was another reason the board didn't accept his version of the story. They said he'd say anything to stay in the competition."

Justin nodded. "Courts of law are different. I'll need a sworn statement from Ivan. Would he give us one?"

"I'm sure he would," Jen said.

"I also want to talk to anyone who was at the workshops you conducted."

"I can get you the names, but we only have two days," she said.

"We'll get this together in no time. I'd like to talk to the cops about setting up a sting and having Carlos arrested for trying to blackmail you."

Jen sat back against the seat and glanced over at Nate. "What do you think about that?"

"I think it's brilliant. It will shut Carlos up and get your good name back."

"That's my thought," Justin said. "Once Cam gets here I want to see if he agrees to us using the club for the setup. We can control it a lot more if he does it in the club."

"Control what?" Jen asked.

"Who is there to witness him threatening you," Justin said.

"Who is threatening Jen?" Cam asked as he walked down toward them.

"Carlos Antonio. And he's threatened the club as well," Justin said. "I'll catch you up on what I've learned."

"Walk with me," Cam said. "It's been a long night and I need a drink… Nate, you don't mind if I help myself, do you?"

"Not at all," Nate said.

His brothers disappeared into the galley and she turned to face Nate. "Thank you for doing this for me."

"You're welcome. I didn't like that guy from the moment I met him," Nate said.

"Why not?"

"He just seems too slick."

"He is that," Jen said. "Not at all like you. I think I thought he was this older chivalrous guy and all the time he was playing me."

"I'm not playing you," Nate said.

"I figured that out in your office," she said. "I'm not playing you, either."

Eleven

Jen wasn't really sure what to say once she was alone with Nate. His brothers had left after working out a rough plan that involved her calling Carlos to the club in the morning. Now it was a little after two a.m. and Nate showed no signs of being tired.

He was wound up and raring to go. Looking for a fight but not with her, for her. The times in her life when she'd needed someone on her side had been rare and she'd always had Marcia, but this was the first time she'd relied on someone who wasn't related to her by blood.

She wanted to pretend that was no big deal and that having Nate on her side didn't mean the world to her. But it did. It meant more than she wanted it to.

"Do you want to spend the night here on the boat or should I take you home?"

"I'd like to stay with you tonight," she said.

"I'd like that, too. Did you call your sister and let her know what was going on?" Nate asked as he handed her another glass of wine.

"No. I don't want to upset her in the middle of the night. I did text her to let her know where I am, though."

"My brothers would be pissed if I didn't tell them what was going on," Nate said.

"She will be, too, but she can't do anything right now and I know she needs a good night's sleep. She's going up against Riley's father in court tomorrow."

"He's a lawyer?"

"Yes. And each time she faces him, it's important to her that she does her best and wins as much as she can."

Nate shook his head. "I get that. Must make it hard on her to see him all the time."

Jen nodded. "The worst part is he still wants to be with her. He just doesn't want to be a dad. Can you imagine that?"

"No, I can't," Nate said.

"Have you heard back from Hutch about the anniversary party?"

"Yes, he's coming in this weekend and you'll have a chance to meet him and work with him."

"I have a few ideas that I think he'll like. I've been listening to his music on my iPod."

"I know. We don't have to talk about the club," Nate said.

"Sorry. I just want to make sure you know that all the help you and your brothers are giving me, it's not wasted."

Nate pulled her close to him and kissed the top of her head. "I already knew that."

"This has been the strangest day. I never thought that Carlos would act like that."

Nate took another sip of his wine and moved around on the bench until he was stretched out lengthwise, and then pulled her close to the side of his body. "Comfy?"

"Yes."

"Good. It's hard to say how someone will react. I had the same thing happen with Daisy."

She tipped her head up to look at him. The night sky was beautiful, clear and filled with stars. The half moon was moving toward the west but the night was still nice. After the turmoil brought on by Carlos, this was exactly what she needed.

"Daisy was my fiancée."

"I didn't know you were married…"

"Never made it to the altar. She was looking for a Yankees player who didn't get injured so when I did, she moved on to the guy who took my place."

Jen shook her head. "That's the most… I'm angry, Nate. She wasn't worthy of you."

He laughed and hugged her close. "No, she wasn't. But I couldn't see it until it was too late. We all fall into relationships like that."

She thought about that. Even Marcia—her smart sister—had fallen for a guy who wasn't everything she'd thought he was. "Why do we do that?"

"I have a theory."

"I bet you do," she said. "What is it?"

"That we find these people when we most need them in our lives. I know for me I needed Daisy when I first started playing because she gave me a reason to get away from the field. She taught me how to relax and enjoy life."

She thought about her time with Carlos. "Carlos gave me a glimpse of what life might be after I stopped dancing."

"But you didn't end up teaching kids," Nate said.

"No, I didn't. I ended up teaching the rich and famous...not so different from kids."

"Ha. I think I'll mention that to Hutch when I pick him up at the airport next week."

"No, don't. I doubt he'll want to work with me if he thinks I called him a child."

Nate laughed. "He will think it's funny. He's a good guy who doesn't take himself too seriously."

"How did you meet him?"

"I met him when we were kids but that's not important," Nate said.

"Yes, it is. I don't want to think about Carlos and what he did. It makes me feel really small and sad. Do you mind talking to me?" she asked. She'd already revealed her vulnerability to Nate tonight—there was no hiding it from him now. She needed to just lie here in his arms and forget that life wasn't perfect.

"I can do that," he said.

He held her closer to him and stroked her hair as he talked about meeting Hutch Damien at boarding school and the trouble they both got in. She enjoyed that. It made Nate all the more real to her and that was exactly what she needed him to be.

Nate carried Jen to his bed and tucked her in before going back up on deck to stare out at the sea. He needed some time alone to figure this out. He didn't like the fact that he'd wanted to physically hurt Carlos. He hadn't been kidding about that.

"Nate?"

He turned to see her standing in the doorway. She leaned there watching him, her hair flowing free around her shoulders.

"Yes?"

"Why didn't you come to bed?" she asked, walking over to join him.

"I couldn't sleep," he said. "And I didn't want to disturb you."

"That is precisely why I couldn't sleep. I like having your arms around me, Nate. I've grown accustomed to you."

He wanted to warn her not to rely on him. That the more deeply they came to care about each other, the more panicked he felt at living up to her needs. But he didn't.

He didn't because she chose that moment to wrap her arms around him. "Dance with me in the moonlight?"

"There isn't any music," he said.

"I will sing for you."

"Can you sing?"

"Sort of."

He chuckled. "I have a stereo system on the yacht. What do you want to hear?"

"What's your favorite song?"

"Slow or fast?"

"I guess I'd say that depends on your mood," she said.

"I love Dean Martin. I know he's not hip, but he is cool—the ultimate cool, you know what I mean?"

"Yes, I do."

"And he sings the perfect songs for holding a woman in your arms."

"I'd have to agree. Dean is a great one for romantic standards. What about a fast song?"

"'Shine a Little Love'…ELO."

"Jeff Lynne is the best. Let's dance to ELO."

"Tonight?"

"Yes. We need something that will make us forget about everything. That's the power of dance."

Nate fiddled with the iPod and the docking station and found "Shine a Little Love." Soon the music was blasting from the speakers and Jen stood on the deck in the moonlight beckoning to him. Her hips were swaying and she drew him closer to her.

She brushed by him and touched him with each move she made, and he felt powerful and together with her. He forgot about his anger toward Carlos—and toward Jen a little for getting herself in this situation.

The night breeze blew across the deck. Jen put her hands up in the air as she twirled and clapped and sang along with the music.

"You're not a bad singer," he said.

"Let me hear your singing voice, Mr. Stern," she said.

He danced closer to her, pulling her into his arms and singing into her ear. She tipped her head up and looked him in the eyes.

He had no idea what he was going to do with her but tonight with the half moon hanging in the sky and calm waters all around them, it didn't really matter.

All that mattered was the way Jen felt in his arms. When the song ended, she took his hand. "Slow dance with me."

He felt her hands make their way under his shirt. She tucked her fingers into the back of his pants and held her to him as they swayed to the sound of the breeze blowing over the bow of the ship and the water that lapped gently against the boat.

And in that moment he knew that no matter what his logical mind might be thinking, he didn't want to be anywhere else. Even with her problems and the complications that Jen brought into his life, she enriched it and gave him something he'd never thought he'd find.

"Thank you," he said.

"What for?"

"For this. For tonight. For dancing with me even though you have every right to distrust all men thanks to Carlos."

She went up on her tiptoes and kissed him. Brushed her lips over his and then held the back of his neck and buried her face against his shoulder. "You are easy to trust."

"Am I?"

"Yes, very easy."

Nate wanted to live up to her expectations of him but he was very afraid that he wouldn't be the man she needed him to be.

But tonight there was no need to worry about disappointing her. He lifted her in his arms and carried her back down to the master suite and laid her in the center of the bed.

"Tired of dancing?" she asked.

"No. I just wanted to make love to you."

"I'm glad."

He took his time taking his clothes off and then removed hers. He kissed every inch of her body and then caressed her until she was moaning his name and begging him to enter her. He was on fire wanting her so badly but he needed to savor it tonight. Needed to take her slowly so that he could wring every ounce of pleasure from both of their bodies.

And he did. When he finally thrust into her, she came in a rush and he followed her with his own climax. He thought he'd never recover from the intensity of it. He curled himself around her when they both came down and tucked her close as they both fell asleep.

Jen was nervous the next day as she waited inside the main room of Luna Azul for Carlos to arrive. This plan had been gone over many times and she knew all she had to do was pretty much let Carlos do the talking. Nate, Justin and Cam were all waiting a few feet away along with a couple of Miami's finest detectives. Thanks to the ceiling's design, if you stood on the far end of it the voices on the other side were clear. It had been designed in the same style as the whispering gallery in St. Paul's Cathedral.

The door opened letting in the bright Florida afternoon sun and Carlos. He walked over to her looking very confident. Now that Nate had mentioned it, he did look a little too slick for his own good.

"I see you changed your mind," Carlos said by way of greeting.

"I haven't," she said. "I just wasn't sure I heard you right the other night. The music was so loud."

"Give me a break. You know what I said. If you don't agree to my terms I will make sure your new bosses know all about your past as well as making you and this club the reason why I cannot teach in Little Havana."

"What are your terms?"

"Since you don't seem willing or able to help me get a job teaching at the dance academy, I think a hundred thousand dollars will do it."

"For what? I don't have that kind of money."

"No, but your bosses do. And rumor has it you are

dating one of them...Nate. I should have guessed that when I met him the other night."

"That's crazy, Carlos. I'm not going to be able to convince Nate to give me that kind of money."

"For your sake, I hope you can," he said. "You cost me my job, Jen, and my reputation."

"That's not true. You cost yourself your reputation. You asked me out and yet they blamed everything on me."

"I did, but the panel found I was at fault as well. I was demoted to the regional circuit, if you recall...I'm not meant to live in Indiana, Jen."

"I'm sorry," she said. And she was sorry. Carlos had tried to make her the scapegoat but she at least had something else to turn to.

"Maybe I can help you get the teaching job here?"

"It's too late. I don't want to teach. And I won't have to. I will expect the money tomorrow."

"I will try..."

"Better use all your wiles, Jen. Don't mess this up or you're going to be out on your ass again."

She shook her head as Carlos turned and walked away. As soon as he was gone she walked over to Nate and the other men.

"You did great," Justin said.

"Do you have enough to arrest him?" she asked.

"Not yet. We will need to catch him taking the money," Detective Elder said.

"I don't think I can get that kind of cash."

"We have it," Cam said. "The cops will arrest him as soon as he takes it from you."

"Great," she said. This didn't sound like her idea of a good plan, but she knew they had to follow the proper channels, or Carlos wouldn't be arrested. And she wanted him in jail.

"So we have until tomorrow?"

"Yes. I will get the money," Cam said.

Cam and Justin stayed with the detectives and Nate led her back to the rehearsal room.

"How are you?" he asked when they were alone.

"Okay," she said because she didn't want to let on how much it bothered her that she was still paying for the mistake of letting Carlos into her life.

"Don't worry about this too much. We will get him. I can promise you that. Standing outside listening to him threaten you—it was all I could do to keep from going after the guy."

She smiled up at him.

"Why are you smiling?" he asked.

"You make me feel very cared for," she admitted.

He nodded. "Don't forget it."

"I won't," she said. "I'm just sorry I brought him here to you guys."

"I'm not. I didn't want you to have to deal with him on your own."

"Me, either," she admitted. "So what are you doing today?"

"Celebrity golf tournament," he said. "Do you have time for dinner tonight?"

"I can't. Alison and I are meeting with the show dancers from the main room to go over some new routines."

"I guess I'll have to try to make it up to the show tonight."

"I'll look forward to it," she said.

Nate left her alone in the rehearsal room. She pondered how close they'd grown over the last few days.

Last night she'd almost told him she loved him. She knew that she cared that deeply for him.

But she had no idea if he was ready to hear that or if he'd ever be. For all she knew, if she ever confessed her love he'd run for the hills.

"You're early today," Alison said as she came into the rehearsal room.

"I couldn't let you keep beating me here."

Alison laughed and they continued joking around with each other as they warmed up. "You're in a good mood today."

"Life is good," Jen said and realized that she meant that. Her life was very good right now. Probably in the place that she'd long wanted to be in. And she was very happy to be finally finding it.

"Life is good with me, too. I talked to my brother today."

"When does he ship out?"

"Another week. We are having a party at the beach house this weekend. Want to come?"

"I might. Can I bring a date?"

"Yes. Who would it be?"

"Just a guy I've been seeing." She didn't want to say that she was dating Nate Stern. They had been keeping a low profile so far. But what kind of relationship could they have if they were both keeping each other secret from their friends?

"Well, let me know if you are going to come."

"I will. Have you done a lot of country-type dancing?" Jen asked.

"Just some line dancing but this tape Ty Bolson and Janna McGree sent calls for more than line dancing."

"Yes, it does. I think we should incorporate some of your line dancing into it. That way our patrons will be able to dance to the music. Not everyone can do a country waltz."

"That's true," Alison agreed.

They spent the rest of the afternoon working on a few routines and then recorded themselves on video for Ty and Janna. "I think this will work better for the event."

All the while, Jen tried to keep her focus on work. Not on the man she was fast falling in love with.

Love.

No. She couldn't love a man like Nate. He wasn't the kind of guy she wanted to fall in love with but it was too late. She already had.

Twelve

Nate stayed out of the club the next day when it was time for Jen to make the money exchange with Carlos. He knew that if he were there he'd once again be battling with himself to go and take Carlos out.

The forty-five minutes he spent outside waiting were the longest of his life. They rivaled even that time when he waited for the doctor to tell him he could no longer play baseball. He knew then that Jen meant more to him than he wanted to admit.

He should drive away. Get the hell out of here and do something that was fun. He needed to go back to his playboy life but he couldn't. Not while Jen was in there dealing with a scumbag.

He waited in his car until the cops escorted Carlos out of the building. It was over. He didn't need to worry anymore about Jen.

He hurried inside and found her. She was visibly

shaken and he wanted to pull her into his arms but he knew that doing so in the club in front of his employees and her coworkers wasn't a good idea. So instead he took her to his home.

"Do you want to hear about it?" she asked, as they entered his apartment.

"No. I don't. I'm glad he's been arrested and I hope you never have to deal with him again."

"Me, too. Thank you."

"Justin did all the work on this one," he said. "Go sit down while I pour us both a drink."

"Make mine club soda. I have to pick Riley up from school this afternoon."

Nate made both of their drinks nonalcoholic and came to sit next to her on the leather couch. "Why are you picking him up?"

"Marcia has a late appointment with one of her clients and the normal sitter isn't available."

Damn. He'd been hoping to have her to himself this afternoon but he forgot that with Jen came her family. She had commitments and a life that had nothing to do with him.

"Do you want to come with me? Riley wants to show you his baseball skills. He's been showing off what you taught him at school."

"Has he?"

"Yes, he talks about you a lot. Marcia said we'd been neglecting him by not having a man in our lives."

Nate thought they probably had been, but two women wouldn't think of having a guy around for a little boy. "I…can't," he said.

He wasn't a family guy and it was time for Jen to realize that. Today had shown him how vulnerable he was where she was concerned and he needed to make sure she never knew the power she had over him. That kind of feminine power had ruined his father.

"Oh, okay. Are you available on Saturday?"

"For?"

"A beach party that Alison's throwing for her brother. She's got a house on Marathon Key. He's being deployed again to the Middle East and she wants to give him a good send-off."

"Alison from the club?" Nate asked. He thought that she was a dancer but he wasn't sure.

"Yes, she's my assistant."

"I think I'd like to attend. Let me know what time it is."

"I gave Alison the night off so she'll be there all day. It's a drop-in party."

"We could take the yacht down to her place," Nate suggested.

"That sounds like fun...do you think Riley and Marcia can join us?" Jen asked.

"I don't think I can handle your entire family," he said. To be honest, he knew he couldn't. They made him feel uncomfortable in his own skin and made him wish...well he was a different man. The kind of man who could make Jen's dreams of family come true.

She shook her head. "Well, okay then. I didn't realize my family was hard to handle." There was an awkward silence.

Jen left a few minutes later to go and pick her nephew up from school. As Nate watched her leave he was struck by the scariest thought he'd ever had. He imagined this was what life would be like if they had a child of their own.

He'd never considered having kids, though he knew that he might someday. But Jen was the first woman he'd met that he could conceive of as a mother to his children.

He quickly turned his attention away from that thought.

That Saturday, back on his yacht after a pleasant but long day, Jen relaxed in the living area in front of the plasma screen TV. Nate was watching the highlights of the Miami Heat game while she rested her head in his lap.

"Thanks for a great time," she said. Realizing that most time spent with Nate was great. In fact, since the mess with Carlos, they'd grown so close that it was hard for her not to tell him she loved him.

Only her fears that he might not love her, too, and that he was still afraid of commitment kept her quiet. But she didn't like to live her life hiding something as big as her love for him. She had started this new life when she'd met Nate and that life was meant to be better than the one she'd left behind.

How could it be if she was afraid to tell him that she loved him?

"It was a fun day. I didn't realize your sister was going to be there."

"She's friends with Alison as well. Thanks for giving them a ride back on your yacht despite the fact that you're uncomfortable with my family. I know Riley enjoyed it."

"It was nothing."

"It meant the world to Riley and to Marcia."

"I'm still not your sister's favorite person."

Jen was aware of that. No matter how many times she'd explained to Marcia that Nate had his picture in the papers with other women for the club and not because he was dating them, her sister just didn't like it. She thought a man should honor his commitment to one woman.

"She just doesn't want to see me get hurt," Jen said.

Nate clicked off the television. After Carlos, he could understand how her sister would be worried about him hurting Jen. And given the fact that he was trying to figure out how to protect himself from caring too much about Jen, he thought maybe Marcia should be worried.

"How could I hurt you?"

Jen sat up, tucking her leg under her body to face him. "By…"

"What?"

She had no idea how to say the words out loud. *By not loving me,* she thought in her head and just kept staring at him like she'd been struck mute.

"You can tell me. Is it the fact that I had my picture in the paper with those two models this morning? You know that was club business and had nothing to do with romance."

"We spend so much time together, I'm not afraid that you are seeing someone else behind my back. Besides, I know you well enough now that you'd tell me if things were over between us."

"Yes, I would. I still don't know what's going on between us, Jen. I keep expecting that we'll grow tired of each other or start to drift apart but the opposite is happening."

Each word he spoke made her feel stronger about the love in her heart and she knew that she was going to tell him how she felt. Tell him that she loved him. And she had the feeling that he'd confess to loving her, too.

"That is exactly how I feel, Nate. I wake each morning looking forward to the part of my day when I know I will see you. And sometimes when you surprise me by dropping by early...well, I get so excited just to see you."

Nate reached out and pulled her close in his arms, hugging her tightly to him. He whispered something into her hair that she couldn't understand.

"What?"

"Some days I just have to see you," he said. "When I know our schedules are busy and we might not have time for each other, I make time."

She smiled up at him, knowing she was doing a horrible job of hiding what she felt at that moment. "I know that's hard for you with your schedule."

"Not hard at all. Now tell me what you were going to say," he encouraged.

"I have been thinking about us all day, Nate," she said. "When we were on the yacht, it made me realize that we could have a family...that we were already becoming a family together and I want that to continue."

"I'm not ready for a family yet," he said.

"I know that," she assured him. Because she did know that he wasn't ready for anything beyond a commitment to her. She wasn't sure she was. She only knew that having Nate in her life and by her side was the most important thing for her right now.

"I meant that I'm looking to my future and seeing a family. That isn't something I'd anticipated. I mean, when I couldn't return to dancing I thought that...I thought that I didn't have a future. But being with you has given me back dreams."

Nate kissed her softly on the top of the head. "I'm very glad to hear that."

"Nate, I'm not sure you are ready to hear this but..." *I love you,* she thought. I love you. Why was it so hard to say those three little words out loud? There was never going to be a better time to say them than right now.

"Yes?"

"I...I love you," she said. She spoke the words softly, and he leaned in as if he had trouble hearing her.

But then his eyes widened and he looked down at her. "What did you say?"

"I love you. You're the man I've been waiting for all my life and never knew that I needed. But being with you has completed me in a way that I never expected. I didn't realize I was incomplete without you. Not until this very moment.

"And I know that you might not be ready to hear those words, but I can't keep quiet anymore. The words have been growing inside me for a long time. My love has been growing for you," she said.

He kept his arm around her, letting her speak, but he had nothing to say. She sat there next to him so afraid she'd just made the biggest mistake of her relationship with him but then he moved and drew her closer to him.

"Jen, you mean more to me than I can say," he whispered against her hair.

He brought his mouth down on hers and she felt in his kiss all that he didn't say. He held her so close and kissed her so carefully that she knew they were going to be okay.

Nate didn't want to think about love or the fact that she scared the crap out of him with that confession. Each day he was with her...he wasn't going to think about that right now. Instead, he was going to do what he did best—make love to her. He wanted to have her lithe body under his again so he'd feel in control and not so unsure of things between them.

He reached for the hem of her T-shirt and pulled it up over her arms. She shifted on the couch to straddle his hips and he leaned back against the pillows looking up at her slim body, the mounds of her breasts encased in the pale yellow bra.

"You have such a pretty body, honey. I can't get enough of touching you," Nate said.

She smiled down at him. "I'm glad you like it. I like your body, too. Will you lean up and take your shirt off for me?"

He did as she asked. And her hands immediately went to his chest, stroking and petting him. "I love the way you feel."

"Do you?" he asked, unhooking the back of her bra and drawing the straps down her arms.

"Yes, I do," she said, shifting forward so that the tips of her breasts brushed over the light covering of hair on his chest.

He shuddered, enjoying the feel of her nipples against him. She shivered delicately and rubbed herself over him as she took his mouth with hers. He let her set the pace for their lovemaking tonight.

He just wanted her. When she took the lead in their passion it was a full-out turn-on. He felt so hard and ready, it took all of his self-control to wait for her.

He put his hands on her waist and shifted on the couch so that he could take her right nipple in his mouth. He teased her with his tongue at first, circling her areola and then gently closed his lips over her and sucked gently.

She dug her hands into his hair and pulled him closer to her. Her legs shifted next to his hips and she rubbed herself against his erection.

"You feel so good, Nate."

He kept teasing her nipple with his mouth and brought his fingers to her other one, plucking at it gently until she was squirming and calling his name.

"I love the sound of my name on your lips."

"Nate."

"Yes, Jen. Tell me what you want," he said. He wanted this to be for her. To show her how much the gift of her love meant to him.

"I want you, Nate. I want to feel the hair on your chest against my breasts. I want you inside me and I want to be together with you—completely yours."

He wanted that, too. He almost came from her words and the remembered feeling of being inside of her. He put his hands around her waist and lifted her up so he could reach between them and free himself from his underwear.

Her hands immediately went to her own pants and she had them off in a minute. Then he was holding her naked in his arms. Here was where he wanted and needed her. Here was where he knew they were doing what they needed to do.

She came down on top of him and let the humid warmth of her center rub up and down his aching hardness. He ran his hands up and down her back and then put them on her hips and drew her up and over him.

She moaned his name again and this time he came up to kiss her neck. He dropped nibbling kisses along the length of it until she shifted, trying to bring the tip of his erection to the portal of her body.

But he made her wait for it. Even though he was close to coming, he wanted this orgasm to be stronger than any of the other ones he'd given her. He wanted her to always remember this night and the passion between them when she thought of loving him.

She reached between their bodies and stroked her hand up and down his length. A drop of precum beaded at his tip and she caught it with her finger and rubbed it around the head of his sensitive shaft. He felt another drop on the tip.

"I need to be inside you now," he said.

"I thought you wanted to wait," she said, a teasing note in her voice.

"Not anymore. You are too much temptation for me tonight."

"Good. I want to be the woman who pushes you over the edge," she said. "You are too controlled in life."

"But not with you," he said. "Never with you."

He didn't like that she made him react the way he did but that was the truth of it. Jen was the one woman he couldn't control his reactions around. Maybe that was why he loved her.

Dammit. Did he really love her? He was trying so hard to keep her at arm's length. Sure he said it was to keep her from getting hurt, but he knew he was also trying to protect himself.

He hadn't the first idea of how to love a woman other than like this. Reaching between her legs he tested her passion and found her wet and wanting. He pulled her down on his rock-hard length. She tipped her head back and moaned loud and long.

He felt his spine tingle with the need for release but he held it off, wanting her to come first. He found her most sensitive spot and stroked it until he felt her inner muscles tightening around his shaft.

"Nate…"

He kept touching her and thrusting in and out of her

body. She grabbed his shoulders and dug her nails into him as another orgasm rocked through her. This time he wanted to come with her and he pulled her down closer to him.

He felt her hot breath against his neck and her velvet perfection around him as he jetted his orgasm deep inside of her. He came long and hard, calling her name and holding her tightly to him.

He held her like that until they both started to drift to sleep and still that wasn't enough. He woke her in the night and made love to her again. And in the morning when he dropped her off at her house and drove away, he knew he was going to have to figure out either how to live with his fear of commitment or live without her.

Thirteen

Jen didn't realize that Nate hadn't told her he loved her until two days later when she noticed that he was avoiding her. She hadn't seen him since that night on the yacht and to be honest, she was worried about that. He'd made passionate love to her and she'd thought...well, he had a hard time with commitment, so maybe that had been his way of showing her how he felt. Instead, she thought it had been his way of keeping her busy until he could get her off his yacht and out of his life.

She had a troupe of local dancers that were working today on the country routine they'd be doing on stage with Ty and Janna. The group was good and she saw some real talent in the bunch. And two of the dancers had that hungry look in their eyes that she remembered from when she was younger. Of course, she'd never wanted to do this kind of dancing but now she wondered why she hadn't. The choreography was fun and she really enjoyed it.

"Let's take it from the top."

She cued up the music and then called out the rhythm to the dancers. She sat in the front of the room watching everyone carefully and looking for mistakes but her mind wasn't on the dancers, it was on Nate. Carlos had been a fling so when things had ended between the two of them, it had been expected. But with Nate…she'd invested more of herself.

That hadn't been her plan but it had happened just the same, and she had no idea how she was going to move on from this. She knew she couldn't just let him drift out of her life. If he wanted things to be over, then she was going to confront him and find out for sure. She needed Nate. She loved Nate and she wasn't going to give up without a fight.

She hit the stop button on the music. "Back row, I need to see more passion from you. Let's start again with the back row in the front. No matter where you are on stage I want you to be one hundred percent engaged. If you can't be, then I will find another dancer to take your place."

The dancers went through the routine again and Jen started to see them come alive in the dance. The same way she knew she'd come alive with Nate. When the session ended and she dismissed everyone, she glanced up to see Cam standing in the doorway.

"Do you have a minute?"

"Yes. What's up?"

She wondered if he was here to fire her. If Nate had sent his big brother to get rid of her she was going to hunt him down and give him a piece of her mind.

"I'm in an awkward position."

She felt tears sting the back of her eyes. "Just say it. I think I know what's coming."

Cam walked farther into the room. "I doubt it. Do you know Russell Holloway?"

"The New Zealand billionaire? No, I really don't run in those circles."

"He wants your number," Cam said.

"I'm not interested in any man but Nate. You can tell him thanks, but no thanks."

"Not for dating you," Cam said. "He wants to hire you. Are you okay?"

She felt stupid when he said that. What had she been thinking? This situation with Nate was making her paranoid. "I'm tired."

"You have been working nonstop on the tenth anniversary celebration and I'm really happy with that, but don't kill yourself for the club."

"I'm not going to. Why do you think Russell Holloway wants to hire me?" she asked.

"He told me he was going to try to steal you away. He heard from some of your more famous students that you are one hell of a dancer and I think he wants to add a stage show to his clubs."

"The Kiwi Klubs are world-famous. I mean, everyone has heard of them."

"I know. It would be a position with a lot of exposure for you."

"Are you unhappy with me?" she asked.

"Not at all," he said. "But it's a good opportunity and I didn't feel right not letting you know."

"I couldn't leave Luna Azul," she said. "Not after all you guys did for me."

Cam handed her a business card. "You make the decision that's right for you. That's what we did when we went to bat for you. After you talk to him let me know what he offered, we might be able to match his offer."

Cam left a few minutes later and she sat down on a stool in the back of the rehearsal room. She wasn't looking to travel the world and be a choreographer for the Kiwi Klubs. But it couldn't hurt to talk to him. Especially if things weren't going well between her and Nate.

She needed to have options and to keep them open. Working at Luna Azul was one of the best things that had ever happened to her—hell, it was the best thing. *Period.* But she knew that if Nate and she didn't make it she wasn't going to be as happy here.

She looked at the business card and wondered what Russell Holloway would say if she called him. She was confused. Life was easier when all she had to do was think about dancing and about the moves that the choreographer had taught her.

She realized how unpredictable life was. She'd had an inkling of it when she'd been forced out of her safe world of competitive dance and when she'd seen her sister give birth to her son all alone.

But this was different. This was her having to make a decision and deal with the consequences. In a way, the impulsive leaping was easier. There was no time to debate the outcome.

But that was what she did all afternoon. Debated with herself. She stared at that card. Even dialed the number more than once and hung up before the call connected. She had no idea what to say to Russell Holloway. Mainly because the one person she could turn to for advice wasn't around for her to get it from. She wanted to know what Nate thought. He was more than a lover to her, he was also a trusted friend and she knew she didn't want to lose him in both areas of her life.

Nate was having a pretty crappy day by the time he got to the club and Cam's office. "What's up?"

"Just some news about Jen. But what's going on with you?"

Nate furrowed his brow. "Speeding ticket, Lori O'Neil is demanding I go out with her tonight or she's going to stop mentioning the club in her celebrity blog and I have to fly to New York to film guest spots on two different shows."

"Sucks to be you and have to go out with a beautiful woman and be on TV."

Nate glared at his brother. "*Don't.* Don't try to shame me into remembering that I have a great life and that I don't have anything to complain about."

Cam shrugged those big shoulders of his. "I guess I don't have to then. Seems you know that you have nothing to bitch about."

"Yeah, I know it but it doesn't change the fact that I'm having a really pissy day."

Cam laughed. "I'll give you that."

Nate threw himself down in one of the large leather guest chairs in Cam's office. On the paneled wall was a portrait of Cam standing in the foyer of their boyhood home dressed in a tuxedo. "Don't you wonder why Dad had those paintings of us done?"

Cam shook his head. "He wanted to create a legacy for us to pass on to our children."

"Are you thinking of having a family?" Nate asked his brother. That very thought—a family of his own— had been on his mind too often lately. "I always believed us Stern men made better bachelors than husbands."

Cam shrugged. "I feel the same. I mean business is a lot easier to figure out than a woman."

Nate laughed. "Tell me about it. Who are you dating?"

"None of your business."

"A secret love?"

"Not really. Not love. Just sex."

Was that what Nate had with Jen? Was it just really good sex? "Have you ever been in love, Cam?"

"One time," his brother admitted. "But it was a long time ago and I was young."

"What did it feel like?"

Cam quirked one eyebrow at him.

"I know that's a silly question but I'm not sure if I know how to love. I mean you and Justin are my brothers and we're blood so I know I can count on you. But a woman...how do I know if I love her or not?"

Cam came around his desk and leaned back on it. "I have no idea, Nate. I wish I had an easy answer for you. But women are complicated and I have no idea how to unravel the mystery of them."

"You're not really helping me," Nate said.

"I know. I'm sorry about that."

Nate thought about the fact that Cam, who was very smart and very sure of himself, wasn't sure of love. Did that mean he had been right in thinking that the Stern men weren't meant for love?

"On a related note to this woman talk—Russell Holloway called me this morning and asked if he could have Jen's number."

Nate went very still. "Why?"

"He's heard some good things about her and he wants to offer her a job."

"I hope you told him to step off."

Cam shook his head. "That's not my call. I gave Jen his message and his business card. It's up to her if she wants to take the job."

Nate didn't agree with his brother but he kept that to himself. He needed to talk to Jen anyway—it was something he'd been avoiding since she'd confessed her love.

He hoped he hadn't driven her straight into Russell's hands by ignoring her the past few days.

"What's the matter?"

"I don't want her to work with Russell," Nate said.

"Then tell her how you feel. I don't know a lot about love but I do know that women are big on talking."

Nate knew that, too. "Do you think talking would have fixed the problems between Dad and Mom?"

Cam walked back around his desk and sat in his leather executive chair. "I don't know that anything would have helped them. They weren't suited to each other."

Nate had thought so, too. Their dad had been so warm and caring and always put Nate and his brothers first, even over his pro-golf career. Made them feel so important to his life. Just the way Nate had observed Jen doing with her nephew. He wondered if he could feel the same about her.

"I don't know what to say," Nate said at last. "To Jen I mean."

"What do you want her to do?" Cam asked.

Nate wanted her to stay, but saying that would let her know that he was as vulnerable to her as she was to him. It would even the scales in the balance of power between them.

He'd heard once that the power in a relationship belonged to the one who cared less. And he was beginning to believe that was true because Jen had all the power. And that was what scared him. He just figured out that it wasn't love. It was the fact that he was going to have no power over anything with her if he admitted how much she meant to him.

And to a man like him, a man used to controlling the world around him, that was almost like saying he'd lose the ability to breathe. It was unthinkable.

"I don't know," he admitted to Cam. "I want her to stay but I'm not sure how to say that to her."

Cam nodded. "Let me know what you decide. I want her to stay for your sake, Nate. If you want Jen don't let her go."

"Aren't you concerned about the club, too? She's a very good dancer."

"There are other good dancers in South Florida, bro, but only one Jen where you're concerned."

Nate knew that Cam had a point and was very glad that his brother had told him about the offer. Even though it was the work day he had a reason to see Jen. Not knowing what Jen was going to do was making him a bit crazy so instead of avoiding her, he sent her a text and asked her to meet him at the park where they took Riley to play baseball. Time to find out what she was thinking and where she wanted her life to be.

Jen was eating an early dinner with Riley and Marcia when she got Nate's text message. Riley had finished his dinner and asked to be excused to the living room.

"Who was that?" Marcia asked once Riley was out of earshot.

"Nate." Jen hoped that he wanted to talk because he'd had time to think about her confession of love and maybe he was ready to move on to the next level of commitment with her.

"What does he want?" Marcia asked.

"To talk, I imagine. Why are you still treating him with distrust?" she asked her sister.

"Why aren't you? He hasn't been around for a few days. Is there something wrong between you guys?"

"I don't know. Can I ask you something…not about Nate?"

"Sure, go ahead," Marcia said.

"I got a rather strange message today."

"What? What was it?" Marcia asked.

"Cam said that Russell Holloway is interested in talking to me about working in his Kiwi Klubs."

"Do you know what you would be doing?" Marcia asked.

"Same as what I do now except you know he has an entire chain of clubs all over the world. My guess is that he'd want me to develop shows for each of the clubs that is unique to their location and then train a dance instructor at each place."

Jen played with the food on her plate. She'd been around and around this in her head and she still couldn't decide if she should call him or not.

"Does he want you to live in New Zealand?"

"I'm not sure where he's going to want me to live. But I like living here with you and Riley."

Marcia sighed and then put on her big-sister face. That serious expression she got when she was about to give advice and make it stick. "You'll never know what it is you are passing up if you don't at least talk to the man."

"Okay. I can talk to him, but what about our family?"

"Jen, we're always going to be family no matter where you live. In fact, you'll probably have a home of your own before too much longer if you stay here. Don't let me and Riley make this decision for you."

Jen shook her head. "This is too hard. It's not like a dancing competition, you know. I loved that and I had to travel but this is my livelihood."

"It's life," Marcia said. "Life is complicated."

"Thanks for nothing," Jen said with a small smile.

Marcia reached across the table and took the fork from her hand. "I wish I could tell you what to do and know that that would be the right decision, but I can't. I won't. You have to do this on your own."

"I know that. I'm just not sure what I want."

"Well, until you talk to him you don't even know what he wants."

"That's true," she admitted. "I guess I'll give him a call. I can't really leave now because of the tenth anniversary celebration at Luna Azul. I'm really busy there."

"Stop making excuses. If you don't want to call him then don't," Marcia said. "But make sure you are making this decision for yourself and not based on me and Riley or even Nate. If Nate loves you he'll follow you wherever you go."

Marcia made it sound so easy. "How do I know if he loves me?"

"Did you tell him you love him?" Marcia asked.

"Yes."

She raised both eyebrows at her. "And…"

"He didn't say anything. I mean he said thanks and that he cared for me and thought I was beautiful…"

"Oh, sweetie, I don't know what to say. What does your heart tell you?" Marcia asked.

Jen leaned back in her chair and thought about her sister's question. Her heart was just focused on Nate. She dreamed about him all night every night. Woke up the past two nights feeling afraid and alone. She wanted his arms around her and she slept better when he was with her.

"That I love him," Jen said. "It all comes back to that. It doesn't matter if he wants me or not, I still love him."

Marcia shook her head. "I know that place and it sucks being there. But you have to make decisions that make sense to you."

Jen had the feeling that Marcia was talking about her own relationship with Riley's dad and not about Jen and Nate anymore. But Jen knew that there were similarities. "Why is love so hard for us?"

"Why should it be easy?" Marcia asked.

"Have I ever mentioned how much I hate it when you answer a question with a question?" Jen asked. "You always do that when you don't have the answer. Why can't you just say I don't know?"

Marcia bit her lip and looked down. "I'm your big sister, Jen, I'm supposed to have the answers. I mean, it's just you and me and Riley and I'm the one who has to know what's going on."

Jen reached for her sister and leaned across the table to hug her. "I'm grown-up now. We can take care of each other, okay?"

Marcia nodded. "What are you going to do?"

"I don't know yet. I'm going to go meet Nate and see where that leads and then I'll decide if I should call Russell. I don't even really know anything about his clubs except their name. And that cute little koala bear logo they have."

"I don't know much about them, either. I will see what info I can find on the internet once I put Riley to bed."

"Thanks, Marcia. I mean for always being here for me and giving me a place to live when I made a mess of my life."

Marcia got up from the table and ruffled Jen's hair as she walked into the kitchen to put the dishes away. "That's what family is for."

Fourteen

Nate sat on a bench under one of the palm trees and watched Jen walking toward him. Her hair was loose and blew in the spring breeze. Her legs were bare beneath a miniskirt and her shoulders bare under the sleeveless top she wore.

She took his breath away. Just looking at her made him realize how much he'd missed her the past two days. And now he had to deal with playing it cool and seeing if she was going to leave him and go work for one of his friends. It didn't matter that he knew she wouldn't be leaving him because she wanted to. He knew he set it up when he'd ignored her confession of love and not told her how he felt. He still wasn't sure he'd be able to do it.

"Hello, Nate," she said, sitting down next to him.

"Hello, Jen."

"Why did you ask me to meet you here?" she asked, pushing her sunglasses up on her head.

She looked tired. Like she hadn't slept in a few days. He wondered if being apart had caused an ache inside her like the one inside him.

He knew he should start off with their relationship stuff but to be honest, the thing that was really on his mind was if she was going to leave him. Leave South Florida for New Zealand and Russell Holloway.

"Have you talked to Holloway?"

She shook her head and pulled her sunglasses off her head and back over her eyes. "No. Is that why you wanted to talk to me?"

"Yes."

"Oh, well, I haven't decided if I'm going to call him yet. I'm really busy with rehearsals for the anniversary celebration. I want to think about this before I make a decision. The last time I did something impulsive…well, let's just say it hasn't worked out as I'd hoped."

"Do you mean me?"

"Yes, I mean you. We haven't seen each other in two days because you have been avoiding me and instead of talking to me about that, you want to know what my job plans are."

Nate knew she had a point and felt that this wasn't going at all the way he'd planned. "It's a valid question, Jen. You are at the stage of your life where you are redefining yourself. I want to know if you are going to walk out the door."

She wrapped an arm around her waist. "Would that matter to you?"

"Of course it would. I care about you, Jen. More than I can say, but it's there," he said.

"I need more than that, Nate. I told you I love you and

that's still true today but I don't want to be like the other women you've dated and see you in the papers all the time and think what might have been. It would be easier for me to pretend that this meant nothing. That I could get over a broken heart by calling Russell Holloway and making plans to leave you and Luna Azul.

"But I know it's not that easy. I didn't fall in love with you on a whim. I fell in love with the man I got to know over the past few weeks. The man who talks to me in the middle of the night and isn't afraid to let me see the person behind the flashbulbs."

Nate had nothing to say to her. Everything she said made her more vulnerable and put more power in his court but he felt like the weak one. The scared one. And one thing he did remember his mother saying was that no woman wanted a weak man. That weakness was the most unattractive thing about any human, most especially a man.

"I want to say the right thing here, honey, but I really don't know what that is," he said, opting for honesty and hoping she'd understand all that he didn't say.

"That is lame. I told you I love you."

"I know that. I'm not trying to be lame."

"No," she said, standing up. "Why can't you say you love me? You can say you want me, but there's no mention of love. Why is it? Do you really not care for me?"

Nate knew this was getting out of control and he had no idea how to fix it. "You are getting upset and that's not the way to have this conversation."

"I'm not upset—I'm disappointed that I've finally found a man I can love and he can't say that he cares for me."

"You know I care for you, Jen."

She shook her head. "That's not enough."

She turned to walk away and he was scared that she might really walk out on him. That this would be the last moment they had together.

"Jen, wait. I can do better," he said.

She glanced back at him over her shoulder. "I know you can. I think that if it is so hard for you to admit how you feel for me then maybe you don't really love me.

"And that's okay. I can see why I'd fall in love with you. But I'm not from your world and you are used to a level of sophistication that I don't have, and maybe my normal life is just not exciting enough for you."

Nate stood up and walked over to her. The Florida sun beamed down on both of them. It was such a nice day he didn't want to let her go. Didn't want to end this relationship with her on a day like today.

"Don't say that. I like the life you and I have. These weeks we've been together have been the most exciting of my life. I've been the closest I've been to peace since I quit playing ball."

"I'm glad," she said, quietly. "I want that for you."

"Give me a chance to prove myself," he said.

She took his hand in hers and then rose up on tiptoes to kiss him. "If you don't love me then there is nothing else to say. I can't do things in half measure and staying with you, loving you while you don't love me, would kill me, Nate. I don't want to live like that."

Jen did what she did best when her life fell apart and that was pouring herself into her work. Almost three days passed before she called Russell Holloway's office and got his secretary. She put Jen through right away.

"This is Holloway."

"Um…hello, this is Jen Miller. Cam Stern gave me your number."

"Jen, it's about time you called me. I have heard a lot of good things about you and I'd love to meet with you in person to discuss an offer."

"A job offer?" she asked.

"Yes. I don't know if you are familiar with my clubs…"

"Mr. Holloway—"

"Call me Russ. Everyone does."

"Okay, Russ. I've heard of your clubs. What kind of job did you have in mind for me? Would you want me to travel to all the locations and train the dancers?"

"Yes, and choreograph new shows. I hope you don't mind but I asked Cam to send me footage of your flamenco show from the club. You are really very talented."

She was flattered. After all the ups and downs and heartache she'd experienced in the past few weeks, it was nice to have a man just say nice things to her. "Thank you."

"You don't have to thank me for telling the truth. Now what do you say?"

"Do I have to give you my answer right now?"

"I can wait a few days," he said. "I'm going to send you a ticket to London."

"Why London?"

"I'm going to be visiting the Kiwi Kensington Klub and you can join me there. Give me your answer then, okay?"

"When is it? I have a lot of rehearsals for the Luna Azul tenth anniversary coming up in May so I can't afford too many days away."

"I like that work ethic," he said with a laugh. "I won't keep you more than a few days."

"Okay. I'll come see you but there is no guarantee I'll take the job."

"I understand," he said.

She phoned Cam and asked for a few days off and then flew to London. She had a glimpse of the life she could have. The Kiwi Klub was bigger than Luna Azul. And it would be very busy and she'd have a chance to reach more people with her dance than she ever had before, but London was cold and rainy and she missed Miami.

She missed Marcia and Riley and she knew in her heart of hearts that this wasn't what she wanted. She'd be taking the job to run away from Nate.

The next morning when she saw Russ she told him her decision.

"I'm sorry, but I guess I'm more of a homebody than I thought I was. I miss my family."

"It's okay. I used to be like that, so I understand. If you ever change your mind, call me. I will always have room for you on my staff."

That was a sweet offer but she knew she wouldn't take him up on it. She was tired of running.

So she flew back to Miami and went back to work. She spent every waking moment at Luna Azul. Trying to prove herself. It had somehow become important to her to make sure she spent as much time there preparing for the tenth anniversary celebration as possible, even though she knew Nate was busy and never showed his face around the club anymore.

One night, when she was alone working on a routine, she heard a voice behind her. "It's time for you to go home."

She glanced at the door of the rehearsal hall and was surprised to see Cam there. He had been riding everyone hard at Luna Azul presumably to ensure that the extra publicity they were getting due to their anniversary celebration wasn't wasted.

"Not yet. I want to practice some of the things from the notes that Hutch sent me tonight. My dancers need to have it nailed before he heads back home."

"They are good and so are you," Cam said. "You need rest. You do know that's important."

"Yes, I know it," she said. But she wasn't going home to rest. She hadn't had a good night's sleep in close to two weeks. Not since she'd broken up with Nate in a sunny park on what should have been the best day of her life. Instead, she'd been sleeping fitfully and never really finding a moment's peace.

"Why are you still here at almost midnight?" he asked. "Why didn't you take the job that Russell offered?"

"I'm here tonight because I'm a perfectionist," she said. "As for your other question, why do you care?"

Cam walked farther into the room and stopped in the middle of it. "I care because my employees are like family to me. I want to make sure that you're okay."

"I'm fine," she said.

"Even though you and Nate are no longer dating?" Cam asked.

"I don't want to talk about this with you," she said. She started gathering up her things. "I'm going to go home now."

"Not yet. Since you're still here and I know my brother isn't sleeping…what happened between the two of you?"

Jen didn't think she could do this. Marcia had tried

to get her to talk but she hadn't been able to. She didn't want to tell anyone that Nate didn't love her. Though his constant partying since they'd broken up was evidence enough.

"I can't talk about this. Seriously, what are you doing here? It doesn't matter how exhausted I am. I can always dance. I'm going to make sure your show rocks."

"I have no doubt about that," Cam said, moving around the room with a casual grace. "What happened to break you two up?"

"Please don't make me rehash this. Why don't you ask Nate?" she asked.

"I can't. Lately he's a total jerk to anyone who tries to ask him anything personal."

Jen soaked up this information. Saddened to hear Nate was having as rough a time as she was. "He seems to be recovering nicely."

"What?"

"He is out partying every night. The women are more beautiful than ever and I saw an interview with him from New York…he didn't seem that broken up about not having me in his life."

"He's good at hiding what he feels. You should know that by now."

Jen crossed her arms over her chest. "I do know that, but I can't make him feel something he doesn't, you know?"

Cam nodded. "He asked me to check in on you. Unlike Nate, you aren't in the papers every day and he has no idea if you are okay."

"I'm okay," she said.

"Truly?"

"No, Cam, I'm not okay. I have a broken heart and I have to be in the same physical location as the man I love and not see him every day. It's torture, but there's nothing I can do about that."

He nodded slowly. "I see your point. So you've been working a lot."

"What else can I do?"

He gave her a self-mocking grin. "You are asking the wrong guy. All I do is work because it keeps me from being alone with myself."

"I'm sorry. At least I can blame this bout of workaholism on Nate."

"True enough. I have my own demons and they don't come from a place of love."

"I'm sorry," she said, realizing the slick golden boy had his own issues and problems.

"Don't be. I have no regrets."

"Me, either, Cam. Tell Nate I don't have any regrets."

Jen gathered her bag and slung it over her shoulder. "Did you want me to take that job that Russell offered?"

"Only if it was something you wanted. I'm not sure what you want from your career here. Working for Russell will give you exposure to a different world of people."

She started walking toward the exit and Cam followed her.

"I do know that. I could maybe even try my hand at dancing in another part of the world," she said to him. "Thank you again for helping out with that Carlos mess."

"I'm just glad that he is being prosecuted and will have to spend some time behind bars. That should make him think twice before he tries to come after anyone again."

"I agree. Thank you."

"You're welcome. I know that you could try competitive dancing if you moved to New Zealand. Why aren't you?"

"Cam, why are you asking me this? Frankly, it doesn't seem like the sort of thing that would be on your mind."

Cam put his hand out and touched her shoulder. "It's not for me. It's for Nate. He can't figure out why you are staying and he's tearing himself up for maybe making you give up the chance of a lifetime."

She blinked at Cam. Nate would try to make this all about him, and in a way it was. "I decided to stop running away. Money and prestige aren't important to me. Roots and family are and I'm not about to give either of them up."

She brushed past Cam and walked down the hallway and then out of the club. She stopped under the streetlights and looked back toward the rooftop. She thought she felt Nate watching her but she knew that couldn't be right. He had already moved on.

Nate watched Jen exit the club and walk slowly up the street to her car. He'd done this every night since they'd been apart. He couldn't stand the thought of anything happening to her. On the nights that he couldn't be here he asked one of his brothers to watch out for her.

Even though they'd broken up, he couldn't let her go. He couldn't get her out of his mind. She haunted him constantly and it was all he could do not to run back to her door and beg her to forgive him. To tell her he'd give her everything he had even though he couldn't love her.

He heard footsteps behind him and turned to see Cam walking toward him. "What did she say?"

Cam just shook his head and leaned against the railing at the edge of the rooftop area. "I think you need to talk to her yourself."

Nate pushed his hands through his thick hair. "Do you think I don't want to? I want to go to her but I'm afraid I'll say anything to get her back. And I don't want to steal her future the way that jerk Carlos did."

"You aren't going to do that. That young woman knows exactly what she wants. She's staying here, I suspect, to be near you."

"What?"

"Yes. She knows that she'd have a different life if she took the job that Russell offered, but that's not important to her. In fact, she told me that the only thing important to her is family and building a life here in Miami."

Nate turned away from his brother. He was tempted to go after Jen right now. But he knew that he couldn't. He knew that if he went now he would have no idea what to say.

"I want her back, Cam."

"Then get her back, Nate. There is no reason for the two of you to be so miserable apart."

"She's miserable?"

"I doubt she's slept in the entire time since you broke up. She's thinner than she was before and she spends every waking hour here at the club rehearsing for the anniversary celebration even though now we aren't sure we are going to be able to have it since the community board is throwing every legal obstacle in front of us that they can."

She was pouring herself into dancing again but this

time the ones to benefit would be the Stern brothers and Luna Azul. "I didn't want that for her."

"What did you want?"

Nate tipped his head back and looked up at the starry sky. "I want her. I need her in my life, Cam."

"What's stopping you from having her?"

His own stubbornness, he thought, and the fact that he was afraid to admit the most important thing of his life.

He loved her.

That was it. He'd known it for a while but had been afraid to define what it was he felt for her. He wanted to pretend that he could control his emotions. Could control how he felt about her but now that they were apart, he'd come to realize he wanted her even more than he'd thought he could.

It wasn't just the physical side of things, though he did long to hold her naked in his arms again. He wanted to make love to her over and over again to reinforce the bonds of love between them. But he also just wanted to sit quietly with her in the morning as they started the day.

"I need your help," he said to Cam.

"Um, what the hell do you think I'm doing by talking to Jen at midnight?"

"Shut up, Cam. This is serious. I need to get Jen back and the only way I'm going to do that is to prove to her that I love her."

Cam nodded. "Tell me what you need."

"I think I need to do this right. I'm going to ask her to marry me. I want to make up for the way I acted when she told me she loved me."

"Again, Nate, what can I do?"

Nate didn't know. He was still trying to figure

everything out. And he was operating from a place of fear. What if it was too late, and she'd already decided he wasn't worth her time? What if she'd fallen out of love with him?

He needed to stack the deck in his favor. "I need her sister and her nephew on my side."

"I don't think I can help you there."

"I know you can't. Will you ask our party planner, Emma, to help you plan the perfect dinner up here under the stars?" Nate asked. The event planner would know what a woman wanted. "Tell her I want the perfect romantic fantasy that every woman has for the night she gets engaged."

Cam didn't seem too happy about the request, but he nodded. "I'll do it."

"Great. Now I have to do everything else."

"When is the dream night going to take place?" Cam asked.

"Tomorrow night. I think…will you call Jen tomorrow and tell her to take the day off. I'm going to arrange for a day at the spa for her…to make up for all the long hours she put in here at the club."

"Okay. Anything else?"

"No, that's it. The rest is up to me."

After Cam left, Nate stayed there on the rooftop garden area making notes and a long list of all the things he had to do. When he had the list finalized he got in his car to head home but found himself in Jen's neighborhood sitting in front her house.

He knew it was crazy but he needed to be closer to her. Now that he'd admitted to himself he loved her, he wanted to go to her and tell her. He needed to try to fix everything that he'd nearly let slip away.

He hoped he could fix it. Prayed that he hadn't

ruined everything by letting her walk out of his life. Because he'd just realized that his mom had been wrong about men and weakness. Sometimes, Nate realized, something like love could make a man weak in one sense but having the right woman love him back could make him stronger in his entire life.

Fifteen

Jen tried to relax at The Boutique Spa at the Ritz-Carlton in Coconut Grove. She'd been surprised when a courier from Cam's office had arrived at her home at ten this morning and told her she was taking the day off. He wanted her pampered and rested before she arrived at the club at five o'clock tonight.

She'd almost turned down the offer of the day off but the courier had told her she had no option. He was to take her to the spa and stay with her to drive her home when she was done relaxing.

She had been massaged and pampered like a princess and she loved every second of it. She had a manicure and a pedicure and a facial and that made her a little sad because she was going to be glowing and beautiful when she left the spa but the only man who she wanted to see—Nate—would never know.

She had to stop thinking of him all the time. But that

was hard. She still had the picture he'd taken of the two of them on his yacht stored on her phone and she found herself looking at it more and more often as the days went by. It was exactly two weeks today since they'd broken up.

She wished she could report that she no longer loved him, but that wasn't about to happen. Her heart was stubbornly sticking to Nate as the man for her. And she didn't know how she was going to keep going until she fell out of love with him—if she ever did.

Her phone rang as she was finishing up at the spa. "Hello, Marcia."

"Jen. I have the afternoon off and thought we could meet up and go shopping," her sister said.

"Meet up where? I have one of the Luna Azul employees who is driving me around today."

"I'll come pick you up and we can go to Nordstrom's and do a little dress shopping. I need something nice to wear to a dinner with the partners next week. I think they are going to offer me junior partner."

"Really?" Jen asked. "I'm so excited for you, sweetie. All of your hard work is finally paying off."

"Yes, it is. And yours will, too. I want to have a girls' afternoon."

"Okay," Jen said. "I'm so relaxed from my massage and treatments. That sounds like the perfect way to continue my day off."

"Good. I'll be there in fifteen minutes."

"Okay. Do we need to get Riley after school?"

"No, Lori is picking him up. The boys have a project they are working on."

Twenty minutes later, Jen was seated in Marcia's Audi convertible driving toward Nordstrom's. They spent the rest of the afternoon trying on dresses and both walked away with two new purchases. She had fun with her sister just laughing and for a few moments she forgot her heart was broken.

That was an eye-opening thing because for the first time, she realized she could still have a good life without Nate. It wouldn't be as happy as it could be if he'd loved her back, but she wouldn't be a miserable woman with her broken heart.

Her cell phone pinged just as they got home and she glanced down at the screen to see it was a text message from Nate.

She hesitated for a moment then opened the message. *I need to see you tonight. Please meet me at the rooftop club at five-thirty.*

"Nate wants me to meet him tonight. Why do you think he wants that?"

Marcia shrugged. "I'm not sure."

"Last night, Cam tried to convince me that I should have taken the job with Russell. Do you think that Nate is going to try now?"

"I don't think so."

"What if he does? What if Nate doesn't want me around anymore and he tried to get Cam to let me go…"

"*Stop.* That's just crazy talk. Get dressed, then see what Nate wants. I think you should wear that red dress you got today and make him realize all he's missing."

Jen glanced over at her sister. "You think so?"

"Yes. Let him see everything he gave up when he walked out on you."

Technically, she'd been the one to walk away. But she didn't argue with her sister. Instead, she sent Nate a text telling him she'd meet him later that night for dinner.

She didn't let herself hope that he might have changed

his mind. Maybe her talk with Cam had convinced Nate's brother that she was sticking around for a while and Nate wanted to make sure they had no hard feelings between them.

She had no idea what he wanted. She only knew that the thought of seeing him tonight excited her. She had missed him. And even if this was the last time they were alone together, she wanted to make the most of it.

She took her time getting dressed. Made sure her makeup was flawlessly applied and then she did her hair. She let the long thick length stay down and when she put on her slim-fitting red dress and the killer stiletto heels she bought to go with it, she knew she looked good.

In fact, she thought she looked as beautiful as Nate had always told her she was.

She walked out of her bedroom and Marcia whistled. "You are going to knock that man on his ass."

"He's used to sexy women," Jen said. She'd never been in this situation before. "I'm almost afraid to go tonight."

"Don't worry. Everything will work out okay."

"Are you sure?" Jen asked.

Marcia laughed and shook her head. "No, I'm not, but I want it to work out for you, Jen. One of us deserves to be happy with the man we love."

She took those words with her as she drove into Little Havana and to Luna Azul.

Nate was beyond nervous as he waited for Jen to arrive. The rooftop garden had been turned into a mini-paradise. There were flowers everywhere and Emma had pulled out the stops by bringing in fountains and trees adorned with twinkle lights and brightly colored Japanese lanterns.

The path from the rooftop entrance to the place where they would dine had been carpeted and rose petals sprinkled to lead the way to him and the table. Nate wore his tux and had a bottle of champagne chilling.

In his pocket was an antique engagement ring he'd found after spending several hours going from jewelry store to jewelry store searching for the one ring that seemed made for Jen.

Now he had everything in place. He'd made this area as perfect as he could and the only variable left was the human factor. The one thing he couldn't control.

In his mind he'd rehearsed what he'd say to her. But he always hesitated when he got to confessing his love. He had no idea how those words were going to sound when he said them and he was a little afraid she'd throw them back in his face.

But he wasn't going to let those fears stop him. Tonight he was going to ask her to marry him. He was going to tell her he loved her and they were going to have a chance at having a life together.

He'd invited his brothers and her sister and nephew to join them later in the evening for dessert and he really hoped they'd all be celebrating.

His phone pinged and he glanced down at the screen. The text message was from Cam.

She's here.

Wish me luck, Nate texted back.

He cued the music on his iPod and had Dean Martin ready to go as soon as she arrived. There was little to do but wait.

As soon as he saw her, he forgot to breathe. She was beautiful. No, she was the most beautiful woman in the world. He couldn't do anything but stare at her. And when she stopped walking and just looked at him, he was afraid she was going to turn and leave him.

"You are gorgeous," he said. "Come over here."

"Thank you," she said, but stayed where she was. "You are very handsome in your tux."

He bowed his head to acknowledge her compliment. "Please come to me, Jen."

She shook her head. "I think I'm dreaming, Nate. I'm afraid to take another step and wake up and find...that this isn't real."

"What would convince you that this is real?"

"You."

He understood what she meant. He went to her and took her hand in his, brought it to his lips and brushed her knuckles with his lips. "Does this feel real?"

"Yes. Why are you doing this?"

He put his fingers over her lips. "I have everything planned. Come over here and sit down and I will tell you."

"You have a plan?"

"Yes, and it's very important to me that this night go right."

"It is?"

"Yes. I want to make up for the pain I've caused you."

He led her to the table and seated her and then turned back to face her. But she was so beautiful he couldn't really think of the words he'd rehearsed. He wanted to be calm and cool but the thought that she wasn't really his was paramount in his mind. He needed to tell her everything.

"I love you."

"Are you sure?" she asked.

"Yes," he said. "Damn. This isn't what I'd planned.

But I want you to know that I have loved you for a long time and I was just too afraid to tell you."

She licked her lips and he groaned wanting to taste her mouth under his.

"Do you still love me?" he asked.

"Yes, I do. I have come to the conclusion that I will always love you."

"Good. I want…" He stopped talking and got down on one knee in front of her. "I want you to marry me. Will you do that, Jen? Will you take a chance on me and go on the best adventure of our lives by spending the rest of yours with me?"

She just stared at him and he realized he'd forgotten to get the ring out. He reached in his pocket but she stopped him by putting her hands on his shoulders. "Are you sure about this? If you ask me to marry you, I'm not going to let you change your mind later."

"I've never been surer of anything in my life. Losing you hurt me in ways I didn't know I could be hurt. The past two weeks have been like trying to live when I can't catch my breath. I need you, Jen. I love you."

"Oh, Nate. I love you, too. I…but will you stay out of the papers with other women?"

"Yes!" he said.

"Then, yes, I will marry you."

He took the box from his pocket and removed the ring from it. He slowly slid it on her ring finger and then drew her to her feet and into his arms. He kissed her slowly and held her close to him.

"Thank you for loving me. You've made my life so much richer by being in it."

She laughed up at him. "You've done the same for me."

They dined together under the stars and talked about

their future. He didn't let go of her hand the entire time and realized he didn't want to let go of her ever again. And when their families joined them for dessert, Nate realized how full his life was. They discussed Luna Azul's tenth anniversary, and their wedding plans.

The future that had seemed uncertain when he'd had to leave baseball now looked so bright. He was positive with Jen's love in his life that he had it all.

* * * * *

COMING NEXT MONTH
Available March 8, 2011

REQUEST YOUR FREE BOOKS!

2 FREE NOVELS PLUS 2 FREE GIFTS!

Silhouette Desire®

Passionate, Powerful, Provocative!

YES! Please send me 2 FREE Silhouette Desire® novels and my 2 FREE gifts (gifts are worth about $10). After receiving them, if I don't wish to receive any more books, I can return the shipping statement marked "cancel." If I don't cancel, I will receive 6 brand-new novels every month and be billed just $4.05 per book in the U.S. or $4.74 per book in Canada. That's a saving of at least 15% off the cover price! It's quite a bargain! Shipping and handling is just 50¢ per book in the U.S. and 75¢ per book in Canada.* I understand that accepting the 2 free books and gifts places me under no obligation to buy anything. I can always return a shipment and cancel at any time. Even if I never buy another book, the two free books and gifts are mine to keep forever.

225/326 SDN FC65

Name	(PLEASE PRINT)

Address	Apt. #

City	State/Prov.	Zip/Postal Code

Signature (if under 18, a parent or guardian must sign)

Mail to the **Reader Service:**

IN U.S.A.: P.O. Box 1867, Buffalo, NY 14240-1867
IN CANADA: P.O. Box 609, Fort Erie, Ontario L2A 5X3

Not valid for current subscribers to Silhouette Desire books.

Want to try two free books from another line?
Call 1-800-873-8635 or visit www.ReaderService.com.

* Terms and prices subject to change without notice. Prices do not include applicable taxes. Sales tax applicable in N.Y. Canadian residents will be charged applicable taxes. Offer not valid in Quebec. This offer is limited to one order per household. All orders subject to credit approval. Credit or debit balances in a customer's account(s) may be offset by any other outstanding balance owed by or to the customer. Please allow 4 to 6 weeks for delivery. Offer available while quantities last.

Your Privacy—The Reader Service is committed to protecting your privacy. Our Privacy Policy is available online at www.ReaderService.com or upon request from the Reader Service.

We make a portion of our mailing list available to reputable third parties that offer products we believe may interest you. If you prefer that we not exchange your name with third parties, or if you wish to clarify or modify your communication preferences, please visit us at www.ReaderService.com/consumerschoice or write to us at Reader Service Preference Service, P.O. Box 9062, Buffalo, NY 14269. Include your complete name and address.

SDES11

USA TODAY *bestselling author Lynne Graham*
is back with a thrilling new trilogy
SECRETLY PREGNANT, CONVENIENTLY WED

Three heroines must marry alpha males to keep
their dreams...but Alejandro, Angelo and Cesario
are not about to be tamed!

Book 1—JEMIMA'S SECRET
Available March 2011 from Harlequin Presents®.

JEMIMA yanked open a drawer in the sideboard to find
Alfie's birth certificate. Her son was her husband's child.
It was a question of telling the truth whether she liked it or
not. She extended the certificate to Alejandro.

"This has to be nonsense," Alejandro asserted.

"Well, if you can find some other way of explaining how
I managed to give birth by that date and Alfie not be yours,
I'd like to hear it," Jemima challenged.

Alejandro glanced up, golden eyes bright as blades and
as dangerous. "All this proves is that you must still have
been pregnant when you walked out on our marriage. It
does not automatically follow that the child is mine."

"'I know it doesn't suit you to hear this news now and I
really didn't want to tell you. But I can't lie to you about it.
Someday Alfie may want to look you up and get acquainted."

"If what you have just told me is the truth, if that little
boy does prove to be mine, it was vindictive and extremely
selfish of you to leave me in ignorance!"

Jemima paled. "When I left you, I had no idea that I was
still pregnant."

"Two years is a long period of time, yet you made no
attempt to inform me that I might be a father. I will want
DNA tests to confirm your claim before I make any deci-

sion about what I want to do."

"Do as you like," she told him curtly. "*I* know who Alfie's father is and there has never been any doubt of his identity."

"I will make arrangements for the tests to be carried out and I will see you again when the result is available," Alejandro drawled with lashings of dark Spanish masculine reserve.

"I'll contact a solicitor and start the divorce," Jemima proffered in turn.

Alejandro's eyes narrowed in a piercing scrutiny that made her uncomfortable. "It would be foolish to do anything before we have that DNA result."

"I disagree," Jemima flashed back. "I should have applied for a divorce the minute I left you!"

Alejandro quirked an ebony brow. "And why didn't you?"

Jemima dealt him a fulminating glance but said nothing, merely moving past him to open her front door in a blunt invitation for him to leave.

"I'll be in touch," he delivered on the doorstep.

What is Alejandro's next move? Perhaps rekindling their marriage is the only solution! But will Jemima agree?

Find out in Lynne Graham's
exciting new romance
JEMIMA'S SECRET

Available March 2011
from Harlequin Presents®.

Start your Best Body today with these top 3 nutrition tips!

1. **SHOP THE PERIMETER OF THE GROCERY STORE:** The good stuff—fruits, veggies, lean proteins and dairy—always line the outer edges of the store. When you veer into the center aisles, you enter the temptation zone, where the unhealthy foods live.

2. **WATCH PORTION SIZES:** Most portion sizes in restaurants are nearly twice the size of a true serving and at home, it's easy to "clean your plate." Use these easy serving guidelines:
   - Protein: the palm of your hand
   - Grains or Fruit: a cup of your hand
   - Veggies: the palm of two open hands

3. **USE THE RAINBOW RULE FOR PRODUCE:** Your produce drawers should be filled with every color of fruits and vegetables. The greater the variety, the more vitamins and other nutrients you add to your diet.

Find these and many more helpful tips in

YOUR BEST BODY NOW
by
TOSCA RENO
WITH STACY BAKER

Bestselling Author of
THE EAT-CLEAN DIET®

Available wherever books are sold!

Desire

SAME GREAT STORIES
AND AUTHORS!

Starting April 2011,
Silhouette Desire will become
Harlequin Desire, but rest assured
that this series will continue to be
the ultimate destination for Powerful,
Passionate and Provocative Romance
with the same great authors that
you've come to know and love!

Harlequin®

Desire

ALWAYS POWERFUL, PASSIONATE
AND PROVOCATIVE

PRESENTING...THE SEVENTH ANNUAL
MORE THAN WORDS™ ANTHOLOGY

Five bestselling authors
Five real-life heroines

This year's Harlequin
More Than Words award
recipients have changed lives,
one good deed at a time. To
celebrate these real-life heroines,
some of Harlequin's most
acclaimed authors have honored
the winners by writing stories
inspired by these dedicated
women. Within the pages
of *More Than Words Volume 7*,
you will find novellas written
by Carly Phillips, Donna Hill
and Jill Shalvis—and online at
www.HarlequinMoreThanWords.com
you can also access stories by
Pamela Morsi and Meryl Sawyer.

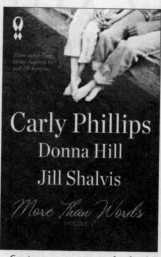

Coming soon in print and online!

Visit
www.HarlequinMoreThanWords.com
to access your FREE ebooks and to nominate
a real-life heroine in your community.

Proceeds from the sale of this book will be
reinvested in Harlequin's charitable initiatives.

MTWV7763CS